JUST THIS

ALSO BY KATRIN HOROWITZ

Power Failures
The Best Soldier's Wife

Just

a novel by Katrin Horowitz

This

Library and Archives Canada Cataloguing in Publication available on request.

ISBN 978-0-9939223-7-4

Published by Quadra Books
Victoria, BC
www.quadrabooks.com

For some obviously bogus reason,
presumably because we have ten fingers,
we find it natural to imagine that life
assumes a completely new character every ten years.

— Louis Menand

The Fifties: The Outskirts of the Middle of Nowhere

See the USA
In your Chevrolet
America's the greatest land of all.

The soundtrack of my childhood. I sang along without giving a single thought to what the words meant.

But my very first memory goes back even earlier—to the summer when I was three or maybe four. A large field, dry and golden. A leafy tree, with a sturdy branch, almost the right height, daring me to climb. I jump, almost get my hands around the branch before falling back. Over and over again. I'm sweaty and breathless, more determined than ever. And then, with a whoosh, I'm hanging from the branch. My feet scramble up the trunk and I hook a leg over the branch. My hair hangs free. With arms and legs I pull myself up and grin at the world below.

Satisfaction. Accomplishment. Mastery. I didn't know any of those words then, but I still remember those feelings zinging through my body. And all these years later, I have labels for them.

I'm perched against the trunk, riding the branch like a pony, when you show up with your bright red hair and your pointy chin. I don't know you. I remember how small you looked. "Pull me up," you say.

And there my memory ends. I can still hear your pleading little voice, but whether I extend my arm or simply sit there in my smug happiness, I don't know. Maybe I don't want to know. I suspect that your witnessing my triumph—and my subsequent failure to pull you up and let you share it—was my first taste of superiority, which would explain why my memory is still so vivid.

Or maybe I pulled you up, because you so badly wanted me to. And maybe, after I pulled you up, you stepped hard on my hand as you climbed to a higher branch. That would explain why my little finger has never been straight. And I could have blocked out all memory of the pain.

After that we became best friends the way little girls do. You stayed with your grandparents every summer and we were almost the same age, so we did things together. There are photographs of us, all skinny legs and arms, you always a little shorter, looking up at me, your chin jutting and vulnerable. The camera catches us with ice cream cones, with badminton racquets, and in one picture that's painfully 1950s sweet, we're playing with dolls on a shady porch with old wicker furniture in the background. The photos are black and white, so I have to imagine your coppery hair. But the camera always caught your longing, the upward tilt of your chin. I can't look at those pictures without hearing your first words to me. "Pull me up."

You might have been thinking those same words when the camera captured your image for today's newspaper. But it's your jowls that catch my eye—those sad pouches of defeated flesh, just hanging from your face. Poor Cynthia, I think, with your jowls exposed on the front page of *The New York Times*. The article itself is all titillation and innuendo—and the promise of more tomorrow.

But those jowls, Cynthia—what were you thinking? Did your handlers convince you that a scarf would look like a cover-up, a tacit admission that you're guilty? Because you've always been good with scarves—like lots of women our age, you use them as stylish distractions that draw the eye away from what's not perfect. Which is probably why, until now, I never noticed the way your face sags. Not that I've been paying a lot of attention over the last while, but I never thought you were the sort of woman who'd let herself go like that. Or the sort of woman who would cross the line. Maybe you didn't— although a part of me hopes you did. Smugness? The phantom ache in my little finger?

Back in the fifties, we knew nothing of jowls, or crossing the line, or much of anything. It was a time when parents—at least my parents—assumed that what their children didn't know their teachers would eventually teach them. They trusted teachers to provide whatever we needed so that we could get on in life. My parents certainly didn't see a role for themselves in explaining the world to us. Instead they found both my ignorance—and my brother Max's, and probably yours too—endlessly entertaining, especially when they had martinis in hand.

And then there was the other new, all-knowing but enigmatic teacher—television. There aren't any photos of our first television set, but as soon as my father brought it home it became a focal point in our lives. My earliest television memory is of a big man who yelled a lot. His name was Senator McCarthy and he thundered against Communists. Why do I remember him so vividly? I'm guessing, but it could be his distinctly nasty, insinuating voice. Or maybe the way he used his bulky body to intimidate witnesses. Or something else entirely, a childish connection that I've long forgotten.

My parents, who thought of themselves as civilized, open-minded Democrats, didn't believe in Communists. They didn't like what Senator McCarthy was doing. Martinis in hand, they would complain about him. But the Senator was too big, too loud and too far away for them to do anything.

To me it was incomprehensible. "He's such a mean man—why does everyone listen to him?" I asked.

"Out of the mouths of babes," said my father. "That's exactly the right question. It's time the other Senators told him he's gone too far. He can't keep doing this. He's ruining the lives of too many good people."

It still bothers me that he never answered my question. And the resentment I felt when he called me a baby hasn't disappeared.

But life moves on. After a while Senator McCarthy wasn't on television anymore, and I suspect I was relieved. I'm quite sure it never occurred to me to ask why he was gone, or whether he would come back.

As best I can remember, *The Mickey Mouse Club* replaced him. It was the first TV program with lots of children who could sing and dance—children who were star performers. And they all wore white turtlenecks with their names spelled out on the back and special Mickey Mouse beanies on their heads, beanies with big round mouse ears. Their exotic glamour helped me forget how Senator McCarthy's ugly yelling upset me.

I was astonished to see that children could become TV stars. I understood, of course, that that kind of glamour was improbable unless you lived in California. Nobody—not me or you or least of all Max—living on the outskirts of the middle of nowhere, was remotely glamorous. Nevertheless—and to the intense irritation of my parents—I learned to sing their theme song in a loud, soulful voice:

> *M-I-C* — *see you real soon!*
> *K-E-Y* — *why? because we like you!*
> *M-O-U-S-E*

And so on — every single repetitive word.

I decided that when I grew up I would live in California—a beautiful place with palm trees, movie stars, swimming pools and an ocean—and that once I was there I would be able to figure out how to become glamorous too. In the meantime I longed for my own beanie with enormous mouse ears. My parents told me I was being silly. "Don't just do what everybody else does," they said. "Think for yourself." Then they turned back to whatever they were doing— cooking or ironing (my mother), reading the paper and smoking a cigarette (my father) or drinking martinis (both of them). I think I knew even then that what they really wanted was for me to think like them.

When you came back the following summer you too knew all the Mickey Mouse Club songs—plus you already had your Mouseketeer beanie. You flaunted it, of course, the way you would later flaunt handsome boyfriends and your more expensive possessions. You wouldn't let me wear it. When I asked, you put a protective, possessive hand on it. "Your head's too big – you'll stretch it." I'm probably imagining your smirk, but I also remember it.

And I remember my guilty pleasure later that summer when a couple of boys, older than us, grabbed it from your head and threw it back and forth until you managed to get a grip on one ear and pull—

and how it tore apart. You screamed at them in rage. They said it was your fault and ran away. And I said something lame like 'that's too bad.' But inside I felt it served you right for being so selfish.

Nevertheless, because there were no other girls my age in the little cul-de-sac where my family lived, and because the highway was a barrier to the rest of the world, every summer I looked forward to your arrival. And I thought of you as my best friend.

Thinking of you as my best friend wasn't my only childhood misconception, although it turned out to be one of the bigger ones. It was also the one I held on to the longest. Looking back, though, I like to think that it wasn't so much you as your grandmother's waffles that kept me playing with you. Whenever we were at your house she would make us waffles with real maple syrup, even if we had both just had lunch, and their warm, sweet goodness filled me with simple happiness—even at the end of summer, when I was anxious to go back to school, and for you to go away. And as I remember the taste and texture of those waffles I find myself wondering how things would have turned out if you had moved in with your grandparents sooner—if the generosity of spirit that was embodied in those waffles would have made a difference. But we can't know, can we? Just one of those idle, irrelevant thoughts.

Unlike my persistent failure to understand our relationship, most of my other childish misconceptions were roughly straightened out quite early in life. Such as my belief that dogs were boys and cats were girls. To me it was obvious. Dogs were smelly and messy and noisy, like my older brother. Cats were the essence of femininity—dainty, elegant, graceful, self-sufficient. They didn't show off like dogs did.

Then came the day that my mother took you and me to the grocery store for ice cream—and she stopped to pet a dog. "Good girl. Aren't you a pretty girl." She embarrassed me with her smiles, with her gushing pleasure, but most of all with her unfathomable mistake.

I tugged on her other hand and said in a desperate whisper, "It's a dog, Mom—you can't call it a girl." I hoped—uselessly—that we could just move on.

Instead she laughed. "It's a girl dog, Michelle. Not all dogs are boys." The dog owner laughed with her, and you made faces at me as if I were the stupidest person in the world. I blinked and bit my tongue and looked away. I refused to cry.

But it didn't make sense. The dumb dog that you too started petting—you even called the dog a 'good girl,' as if you were some sort of small grown-up—was just as smelly as my brother Max or any other dog. Nobody enlightened me. Sex education hadn't been invented yet.

And then there was youth in Asia. One night, as my parents, my brother and I sat around the kitchen table eating dinner—liver and onions, my most hated dinner ever—the conversation turned to youth in Asia. They didn't usually talk about Asia. Most dinner conversations were about American politics. They didn't like the President, even though he looked a lot like your grandfather, who they did like. But this particular dinnertime all three of them were excited about youth in Asia. It had something to do with keeping the population young by helping sick old people go to sleep easily. They said it was like putting dogs to sleep, which was the humane thing to do, although I'd never seen a dog have any trouble sleeping. I stopped pushing the liver around my plate and under the mashed potatoes long enough to ask if we had youth in America too. Not that I got an answer, other than their amusement, but it became one of the signature family stories, retold every Thanksgiving and Christmas. And you smirked every time you heard it.

Anyhow, you get the idea. Or maybe not. I don't think I was really as clueless as that. I was an American, after all, so my birthright included an unflagging belief that life should—and eventually would—be fair. A belief reinforced every morning at school when we repeated the Pledge of Allegiance, which promised us *One nation, under God, with liberty and justice for all.*

And sometimes I got things right, despite the best efforts of the adults in my life. I'm still proud of the first time I stood up publicly for what I believed in. It was a sunny fall afternoon—I was late because I had gone home for lunch and hadn't bothered to hurry back. The teacher was explaining something and scowled at me as I sat down at my desk.

"The important thing," she was saying, "is to get your whole body under your desk, and to cover up your head with your arms, like this."

She crouched down, her skirt flaring around her shiny black high-heeled shoes, ducked her head and covered it with her arms. She nearly lost her balance, and I covered my mouth to muffle a snicker.

She stood up again and glanced at me suspiciously, but then gave a small smile. "If you happen to be wearing high heels, it's probably a good idea to take them off." With her permission, this time everyone laughed.

"Seriously, though—and this is serious—getting your whole body under your desk is the best way to protect yourself from radiation. And make sure to close your eyes, or you could be blinded by the light from the explosion."

She was talking about what would happen if the Soviet Union dropped a nuclear bomb on the United States. I looked at my desk—a square of wood, four metal legs, a few screws holding the whole thing together. She was scaring me. I thought of the images I'd seen on television of the devastation that a nuclear bomb caused. The pictures of Hiroshima in *Life*. A city blasted out of existence, nothing left but dust and rubble.

I imagined my sturdy school building exploding into chunks of brick and shards of glass. A landscape of devastated buildings. And twenty-four crouching children, each covered by a square of wood. I had never heard of cognitive dissonance, but I was caught in its absurdity.

"How can hiding under a desk save us from a nuclear bomb?" I blurted out my question without raising my hand. Then everyone started talking.

"My parents are building a bomb shelter. We'll be safe."

"But you have to be home when the bomb hits, otherwise you'll be dead too."

"Aw, we'll get some warning—we'll have time."

"Are you going to let your friends in too?"

"We can't do that—there won't be enough air or water or anything for us if we do that."

"I don't want to be in your smelly old bomb shelter anyway."

"What if one of your parents can't get back—then would you let a friend in?"

"Yeah, that's what you should do—you shouldn't let the space go to waste."

The teacher whacked her long pointer on her big desk, a solid desk with drawers and a cubbyhole someone might actually be able to hide in. "Children. Children. Quiet. Right now. We can't have everyone talking at once. Quiet!" As her voice got louder, we became quiet.

She frowned at me, or maybe all of us, and spoke in her slow, stern voice. "We are not talking about bomb shelters right now. We're talking about how to be prepared if the Soviet Union attacks the United States. We will practice hiding under our desks because the government says that you have a much better chance of survival if you're protected from the initial blast."

I imagined a bright flash and a billowing mushroom cloud. A wave of hot wind blowing radioactive rocks and dust at us. I imagined all of us with clothes and flesh melting off our bodies, like the pictures of children mutilated by the Hiroshima attack. I imagined how much it would hurt.

I couldn't stop myself from saying, "So that we can die a horrible death later instead of right away?"

"Michelle, you're not being helpful. We're talking about how to keep all of you alive." She looked flustered.

I was belligerent. "I don't care. I won't hide under my desk. I don't want to live after a nuclear bomb attack." And in that instant I realized that I wasn't scared anymore—at least not in the same panicky way I had been a moment ago. If grown-ups were going to be stupid enough to drop bombs on children, then there was no reason to listen to them. They were wrong.

I think that's when I first started writing poetry. The feelings poured out of me in a jumble—crayoned words artfully arranged on sheets of paper, the colors as important to me as the words. I remember forcing myself to save black and red for the most important words. I have an image of a particularly passionate page with only the word CRAZY on it—in alternating red and black letters—my definitive judgment on the world, or school, or my family. And I remember tearing that piece of paper into tiny little pieces, as if I were guilty, as if I had crossed a line.

As I got more serious about my poems I lobbied my parents for the full box of sixty-four Crayola crayons. I longed for nuance, more shades of meaning interpreted in more choices of blues and greens, pinks and oranges. I now think I was striving for purple poetry—the ultimate achievement—beyond even purple prose.

My parents, to my dismay, were not sympathetic to my poetic endeavours. "What would you do with that many colors? You'll never use most of them, and you'll want another box as soon as the black or the red breaks anyhow."

"No I won't. I need them."

"You've got enough."

"No, I don't—I need more colors—the little boxes are for babies."

"Michelle, no. It's a waste of money. Go out and play."

I think back to those times and can only sigh. How much could a box of crayons have cost, even the big one I lusted after? Less than a bottle of vermouth, I think, still capable of a little anger at my parents' thoughtless rejection. And then I laugh, because—just like that—I understand why I always buy large new packs of colored markers when my granddaughter comes to visit, and why it gives me such pleasure to see her use them for her elaborate dinosaur drawings.

By the time the fifties came to an end, the threat of nuclear war had retreated—soon after, the government stopped above-ground nuclear testing, although the fallout in our teeth and bones lasted for another eighteen years on average, if you believe the scientists who did the research. Senator McCarthy was conveniently dead. He had become an embarrassment—no one talked about him anymore. President Eisenhower, the president my parents never liked, warned the country about the military-industrial complex—a warning no one took seriously because he was a lame duck President—he couldn't run again and that made him irrelevant—and then he disappeared too.

And I no longer wrote my poems in crayon. The later ones were, I suspect, less purple than my earliest efforts. I can only find one that survived, written on cheap, yellowed paper, frayed at the edges. I can still see the smudge marks left by the eraser that I used extensively, and the faint pencil lines that I traced in ink. But the erasures, the tracing—and the little flutter I feel in my chest—suggest that this poem was important to me.

Nature's Kingdom

Where trees cast their shadow, upon the frozen land
Underneath the wide blue sky the desert lays its sand
Beneath the clear waters, amongst the rainbow fish
Someone has a dream, of everything they wish

It's the last line that catches my eye, with its hint that the dream, the thing the elusive 'someone' in the poem wishes for, is just this: the ability to love the natural beauty of the world. Not a bad poem, I tell my much younger self. Or maybe I'm just being self-indulgent. Even after all these years I still can't achieve the perspective or the detachment to critique my own work.

Anyhow, as I was saying, the fifties eventually came to an end. By then I was twelve years old, and a lot of my former naiveté had disappeared. In private I thought of myself as a poet. In public I was a baseball fan like my parents and brother, watching the Yankees games on television, pretending to do my homework and really writing poems about baseball and Bobby Richardson's eyelashes.

Does anyone else even remember Bobby Richardson? Most people, you included, paid attention to the stars—Mickey Mantle, Roger Maris, Whitey Ford, Yogi Berra—names that a few people might still remember. But Bobby Richardson was my guy—the Yankees' second baseman—and he looked perfect, right down to his long eyelashes. I was disappointed when I learned later that he was devoutly Christian. I thought of myself as not just a poet but also an intellectually tough atheist. Even perfect eyelashes weren't going to change that. Bobby and I had no imaginable future together.

Because I felt I had become pretty sophisticated—and a lot smarter than most of the adults in my life. You were a few months younger and a year behind me in school, so I thought I was smarter than you too. But I was wrong. We were smart in different ways, and about different things. What you were really good at was knowing how to manipulate people. Getting your grandmother to make us waffles was only a starting point. You had your eyes on bigger conquests. I, on the other hand, as you can perhaps tell from my poem—and despite my dusting of sophistication—I was a secret romantic.

The future ain't what it used to be. — *Yogi Berra*

EARLY FRIDAY: New York City

It's early, maybe three-thirty or four, still dark. You're asleep under your duvet with its leopard-skin pattern, but the rumpled look of your bed and the disarray of your now-blond hair on your charcoal grey pillowcase both indicate that you had a hard time falling asleep. Not surprising, given what you have to face in the morning. Even though you refused to let the *Times* reporter interview you.

There's a sheen of sweat on your forehead, although the room isn't particularly warm. You roll over, fling your arm over your head, make an indeterminate sound, and continue sleeping. In the gloom, your dark fingernails look like leopard spots that escaped from your duvet.

> I pledge allegiance / to the flag:
> *I plug elegance / two thief rag* — *Michael Magee*

EARLY FRIDAY: Berkeley, CA

It's after midnight when I wake up. A much-needed rain is falling, and the wind is blowing the curtains. Alex, who's the good sleeper, doesn't move. I get up, close the window, wipe the sill with a towel, and then go downstairs to get a better view of the storm.

There's a bay window in our living room that offers the best storm watching. We furnished it with a small table and two comfortable chairs that swivel—inward for extra seating during parties, toward each other when Alex and I relax and talk over a glass of wine at the end of the day, and outward for a wide angle view at times like this, when a rare thunderstorm lights up the sky. I settle down to watch with a sigh of contentment.

The rain won't last—it won't be enough to turn the Berkeley hills green again—but it's better than nothing. I imagine my pores inhaling the moisture like a cactus, storing it up for the dry months yet to come. If Alex were awake, I'd be tempted to dance naked on the deck in hopes of making the rain last. But he's not, and I'm not foolish or reckless enough to expose myself like that.

Instead I ponder my poor garden, which is too dead to benefit. Only the drought-resistant weeds are left to soak up the water and make more weed babies. And I think about *The New York Times* and what dramatic revelations about you they're planning to expose. I could turn on my computer—it's late enough—I could search the web, find out what's new. But that would wake me up too much. The story's not going to go away. I can wait until morning for the next instalment.

After a short while the rain and wind stop. I head upstairs to open the window again to the cool night air.

In bed I snuggle up to the warm welcome of Alex's back and legs and fall asleep.

> With liberty and justice for all:
> *impunity / and just this / for all* — *Michael Magee*

The Sixties: The Outskirts of the Middle of Nowhere

I think of the sixties as our Technicolor decade. It wasn't just that it was the decade you became a full-time part of my life, or that our adolescent hormones made everything larger, brighter and achingly melodramatic, although it was certainly all those things. There was more. From the moment the country elected a young, handsome President with hair like amber waves of grain, with his elegant wife, with their children as glamorous as Mouseketeers, life felt saturated with symbols and metaphors. Even in the anonymous suburb of the unimportant city where I lived with my parents and Max, everyone understood that America was the best nation on earth—and that our generation, the babies of the country's post-war exuberance, would make everything even better.

Looking back from a more cynical time it's hard to believe that there was ever a moment when an entire country expected great things of the next generation, but the way I remember it, from the time President Kennedy was elected until the start of the Cuban Missile Crisis, we basked in a golden age of unfettered optimism. I know now that if I had been a black woman living in an inner city neighbourhood, or if I'd been a soldier sent to fight a growing war in Vietnam, or indeed if I had been anything other than a teenaged white girl in a middle class family, that the start of the sixties would have felt different, but if you look back at old issues of *Time* or *Life*, you'll see my teenage optimism reflected there. I didn't make it all up.

You arrived that summer wearing clothes that no longer fit. Your mother was driving a rusty old car that I'd never seen before and your father never came at all, not even for the Fourth of July weekend. Your grandfather tried to take his place—he even wore your father's old Bar-B-Q King apron—but it wasn't the same. There was no boisterous teasing, the few jokes were bland and the hamburgers dry.

The word 'divorce' was whispered around our house, although never at the dinner table, never when they knew I was listening. But I could tell they felt sorry for you and your mother, and they were extra nice to you when you came over for supper.

It must have been a few days after you and your mother drove up to your grandparents' house in that noisy old rattletrap that my mother came into my bedroom carrying two cups of coffee. Hers was black and half empty; the one she brought for me was sweet and milky and fragrant. She sat down on the side of my bed and stroked my hair.

She told me how hard it was for you and your mother, that your life was harder now, and although she didn't say how, she kept repeating the words —hard, harder. And she told me that we had a responsibility to help people who needed help—that I should be especially nice to you, because of the situation. And that she wanted to give my outgrown clothes to you, and to be sure not to say anything about it, so as not to cause embarrassment. "You do understand, don't you?" she said. And of course I said yes, because that was what she expected, even though I had no idea what she was talking about. The coffee she had brought me was warm and comforting, and I wasn't awake enough to ask any questions.

It was creepy to see you wearing my old clothes. Somehow you made them look fresh again —whether it was the way you added a scarf or a belt, an unusual combination of colors, or maybe just that your long red hair made you look special, no matter what you wore. You were so pretty—and you never looked like you needed help, despite what my mother said.

That summer we were both absorbed in how to make ourselves look prettier. *Seventeen* was our aspirational magazine. The ads told us which brands of makeup we should buy and the articles told us how to use them to enhance our beauty. At least that's what the magazine called it. But the effect we really wanted was pretty. *See the pretty girl in that mirror there*, we sang in the privacy of the locked bathroom, after the application and re-application of all our makeup. The pink tiles lent depth to our voices as we twirled around in that small space. And then, to pretend that we weren't yet serious about becoming women, we would giggle and hug each other. That summer we saw *West Side Story* at least three times, and every time, when we came out of the theatre, we could only talk about living together in New York City, about Tony falling in love with us, about wearing those flouncy skirts that insisted on dancing, and—we only whispered this part—about having the bodies to fit into them.

We learned every song. When you called me after dinner, I would run for the phone, knowing it was you. And you, knowing I would pick up, just started singing. Depending on the kind of day it had been, you could be silly: *Officer Krupke, we're very upset* . . .   Or romantic: *There's a place for us* . . . ' Or dangerous and sexy: *The Jets are gonna have their day. Tonight* . . . ' followed by *Tonight, tonight, won't be like any night* . . . ' We loved those songs, we loved the movie, we loved every character in it. We experienced that movie as real life, only better: immediate, passionate, vulnerable, emotional—living in Technicolor. It was nothing like the boring, eventless holding pattern we really existed in, playing with makeup and waiting for something interesting to happen on the outskirts of the middle of nowhere.

If you looked at it from a different perspective, though, I guess you could say that what didn't happen in our world was more interesting than what did. Like that Sunday around the end of July, when your father was supposed to pick you up. You refused to have anything to do with me, even though I showed up on your front porch with my brand new nail polish. All day you did nothing but wait for your stupid father on your stupid grandparents' stupid porch, lifting your pointy chin to look at every passing car, even the ones that were going way too fast to stop, and then dropping your head back down to the book you pretended you were reading. And the whole time you looked so pretty, all dressed up in the crisp, starched gingham skirt that had been mine the year before.

Looking back, I think I had a sense of your vulnerability. The way you raised your chin, and then how it fell back, slack. I must have thought about the words my mother had used—hard, harder. I might have asked myself if I would care if my own father didn't show up— and how much I would care. But what I remember most clearly is how irritated I was that you were ignoring me and my lovely new nail polish—after all, I had chosen the most sophisticated shade of red I could find, the red that had presence without being gaudy and cheap, because I was sure you would love it.

That night I overheard my parents talking about you. Hard came up in that conversation too. And maybe I began to understand what my mother meant by hard, and harder, although real understanding was far away, probably impossible, certainly at that point in my life.

"Cynthia's going to have a hard time of it if this gets out."

"What do you think we should do?"

"We can't bring her back—and we can't force her to do the right thing. So all we can do is act like everything is normal."

"But why would she run away like that? Where's her sense of responsibility? And why in the world did her father say he was coming and then not? Seeing her waiting for him just about broke my heart."

"Some people just shouldn't have kids." My father, as usual, had the final word. I could hear him turn the page of his newspaper.

As quietly as I could I went back upstairs.

We eventually painted our nails—toes as well as fingers—with my red nail polish and I remember you saying how much you liked the color. You never talked about your father not showing up, or the fact that your mother wasn't there anymore, or that the only reminder of her was the crummy old car parked next to your grandparents' garage. And I never remember you looking vulnerable again. Not until now.

I find myself wondering whether during that long-ago summer I should have asked about your parents, whether you needed to talk about what had happened. Would an offer to listen—to give you a chance to rant against the unfairness of it all—have made any difference? But no, although it feels like the easy answer, I think not—my question itself is rooted in a different, more confessional time. Back then we believed in the gods of privacy, of saving face and keeping up appearances. We believed in shame, and that it should be kept hidden. And now that I think of it, I'm convinced that you still worship those same gods. I can't imagine you confessing to what really happened at the Cancer Foundation. But I can imagine you very angry about all the nasty publicity you're getting.

Anyhow, the point I wanted to make is that, despite your personal circumstances, like the rest of us, you too rode high on the wave of hope that surged through the country. Looking back, it seems to me that you knew even then that your survival depended on covering up your humiliation over your mother's rejection and your father's absence. And you learned all too well how to project an optimism that I now suspect was entirely phoney. But there was nothing phoney about the determination that went with it—that was pure Cynthia. You did so well in school that within a year or two of moving in with your grandparents you skipped a grade.

From then on we were in the same class—and we turned into what I can only describe as a weird two-headed entity. Michelle-and-Cynthia. Cynthia-and-Michelle. Even our report cards looked identical. We were the smart girls, a fact that should have been totally obnoxious but wasn't because Cynthia-and-Michelle had a reputation for sarcasm. I think it started when Mr. Lewis, our biology teacher, said something truly dumb. We looked at each other and in one voice said, "Mr. Clueless." The name stuck, of course. And then there was the other teacher, the one with the clunky hearing aid behind his ear. You and I took turns answering his questions, more and more softly, both of us looking blandly innocent as he adjusted and readjusted the volume control attached to his belt. The rest of the class sat back and waited for the punch line, which got funnier with repetition. They always laughed when, as he reached maximum volume, we shouted out the next answer in unison. As Cynthia-and-Michelle we learned early on that if you make people laugh they will forgive you almost anything—awful behavior or even intelligence.

I cringe now, thinking about how mean we were, how callously we targeted our weakest teachers, all for the cheap satisfaction of a laugh. I wonder whether it was you or me that first realized that the kind of men who became teachers in those days—at least the kind who worked in our unremarkable high school—were losers. Losers who would never expose their humiliation to anyone in authority, so we were safe. I'd like to think it was you—after all, you're the one who's accused of illegal behavior, not me, so it stands to reason that you started practicing early on. But that feels too simplistic, too deterministic—it's too easy to draw a straight line from then to now. Life is loopier than that. For the time being, let's just say that our double-entity identity, the whole Michelle-and-Cynthia thing, played its part—that we formed a two-headed, four-breasted creature, oddly smart, that got away with bad behavior because we were funny—and that we worked at being an anomaly so that nobody would see us as a threat.

The idea, of course, was for people to think that our only goal was to entertain them. And the Michelle-and-Cynthia Show was a way to make school less boring. But it was also camouflage for our ambitions, which we talked about with earnest intensity only when we were alone. We were both convinced that getting A's was our only way out—we couldn't imagine any other escape from the suburbs. With all our A's we would make it to Los Angeles or New York City. It was our deepest and dearest secret.

What we would do when we got there we never quite decided, although we tried on different ways of being grown-ups. Stewardess appealed for a while, because of the snazzy uniforms and the chance to fly to Paris, but then one day you said it was like being a waitress in the sky—I suspect that line came from your grandmother—and we both shuddered at the idea of turning into anything like the old waitresses at the Park Diner with their thick arms and sore feet. We scratched stewardess off our list.

I insisted that we needed jobs that were more intellectual. "Movies are so-o-o-o shallow. They're all about breasts." We giggled, although your breasts were already more impressive than mine, and my giggle may have had some envy in it. Shallow was my favorite judgment, both at school and at home, and I used it to show how sophisticated I was. You, I think, were less wholehearted about the shallowness of the movies.

"Being an actress in the theatre is more artistic," I said. "You have to have talent—it's not just about breasts." I'm probably imagining your look of deflation.

"How about being a reporter—working for a newspaper?"

"Or do you think publishing would be more elegant? Nobody

throws a book away after one day."

"Maybe advertising? Wouldn't it be fun to dream up ads and get paid for it? And wouldn't everybody be amazed when they saw our ads on television?" We spent the rest of the afternoon making up jingles about the virtues of cars and candy bars and then staging them in front of the television.

How innocent we were, I can't help thinking. How little we knew of how the world works.

Meanwhile, we considered ourselves lucky that staying at the top of the class wasn't particularly time-consuming. Most days after school we would sprawl on the living room carpet, turn on the television, and do our homework during the commercial breaks in our favorite programs. Or share our latest fantasies of a hazy, amorphous, but always glamorous future. Sometimes you stayed for supper and we'd keep watching television and advancing our studies until my parents said it was late and sent you home to your grandparents.

We were finishing our history assignment, still parked on the carpet surrounded by our books and papers, when the Cuban Missile Crisis started. The President filled the television screen. He showed us fuzzy pictures that he said were Russian missile installations in Cuba. He showed us other pictures of Russian ships carrying missiles headed toward Cuba. He declared a blockade to stop any ship with military cargo. And he said that if a missile was launched against the United States, then he would hit back with a 'full retaliatory response.' We were on the brink of nuclear war. We could all be dead by tomorrow.

Disbelief. Incomprehension. Words I thought I knew, but until then I had never understood how they could twist my gut. The whole thing might have been a dramatic scene in a movie, the kind where the music in the background ratchets up the tension. Except that there was no music, and the President was the real President. And because the tense moment went on and on, which it never does in a movie because that would be boring.

When I looked at you your eyes seemed focused inward, with a glaze of distress. And my parents in their easy chairs looked grim. My mother rigid, barely breathing. My father, oblivious to the cigarette that grew a long log of ash down toward his fingers. I watched the ash fall to the carpet; understood that such a small mess no longer mattered. He stubbed the butt out when it threatened to burn his fingers, his eyes never moving from the screen.

Max, watching from the doorway, muttered something and retreated to his room. I heard his door slam shut. I felt his anger. And realized, I think for the first time, that I really, actually loved him, even the smell of him, that it hurt to imagine him dead. That I shared his anger at being forced to face how irrelevant our lives were. That I hated that we lived in a bizarre world where the big guys with their resolute expressions and stiff posture talked in reasonable tones about the steps toward global annihilation.

Years later, when his first child, a little girl, was born, late in the night when it was only the two of us left in his living room, we opened another bottle of wine and talked about our different childhood memories. And how odd it was that we remembered such different things, as if we had grown up in different houses and with different parents. Whether girls' memories were always different from boys'—what his daughter would remember when she grew up.

There was only one memory that Max and I both shared—our helpless, frightened anger that dark night in October when President Kennedy announced that the world was on the brink of oblivion. But the older brother/younger sister differences persisted. He told me about punching his books and his desk until his fists were sore, how he nearly smashed the mirror too, how he couldn't get over the unfairness of it, especially that he would never have real sex. With a wry smile he admitted he spent that night imagining a naked Marilyn Monroe in his bed—and that it didn't make him feel any better.

I told him how I felt like it was the end of everything. About refusing to go to school, because they would be pointlessly practicing hiding under desks—or worse, pretending that our old world of homework assignments and tests still had some meaning. About claiming to be sick and spending the day in front of the television, watching the two most powerful nations in the world taunt each other with their bullying, bluffing and browbeating. About being repulsed by how repetitive it all was, about me wanting the end of the world to be more dignified. But still needing to be a witness when the first missile was fired. So I kept watch every day until finally the Russian ships turned around and the finger was lifted from the red button.

As we drank the last of the wine, I told Max about the ghastly poem I wrote and rewrote during my days in front of the television, comparing the ash falling from Dad's cigarette with nuclear ash covering the world. And he said that he'd do his best to convince his wife that their daughter's middle name should be Ashley, that it was a secret family name. It didn't happen.

What about you? How did you deal with your feelings? I can still remember how taut and pale your face was in the cold light of the television screen. But after that I forgot about you. I was consumed by my own distress until it was over. I don't remember you leaving that evening, and in the following days I didn't think to call you. I never asked whether you bothered to go to school while the crisis unfolded.

Not that you asked where I had been either. I could be melodramatic and hypothesize that our friendship started fraying ever so slightly then. But there were at least a few more loops left, times when we would fall apart and times when we would come closer together again. I'm probably imagining that we never shared our secret dreams and fears again after the Cuban Missile Crisis.

What I remember vividly is that thirteen months later President Kennedy was dead in Dallas and the Cynthia-and-Michelle Show was over. Not that there was any connection. It's just that I remember being all alone in front of the television—you weren't there, and neither were my parents or Max—only me, watching the aftermath of his shooting and remembering how I felt back when the world was about to blow up. I was still alone when I saw Lee Harvey Oswald, the man accused of killing the President, shot to death on live television.

Disbelief. Incomprehension. Or, to borrow from Yogi Berra, *déjà vu all over again.*

But this time the world wasn't coming to an end. What had ended, although the full realization was still far in the future, was the shared dream of what America could become—the national dream, *one nation, indivisible, with liberty and justice for all.* The gaps that separated us seemed to grow bigger again, more painful, more strident. We became more passionate about our differences. Blacks first, then peaceniks, then women. Rich versus poor, urban or rural, east or west, liberal elites, conservative populists—like the K-Tel food chopper they advertised on late-night television, we sliced and diced ourselves into clumsy chunks and incompatible sizes. *Things fall apart; the centre cannot hold.*

Like comedy before tragedy, the Cynthia-and-Michelle Show fell apart sometime before Kennedy was killed. First gradually, and then all at once. The way I remember it, at the end of tenth grade you and Grant—Grant with the dark hair that fell over his forehead and drew attention to his intense blue eyes, Grant with his sexy smile and preppie clothes, Grant who was the only boy who was both smart and cool, who announced he would go to Harvard, who everyone knew would be rich and successful—anyhow, at that point the two of you were kind of, sort of, a couple. At school dances you danced only with each other and you made out in the dark outside the door, although he never gave you his ring or anything like that.

Then he went away for the summer. You stayed home with your grandparents, as you always did, and you acted as though we owed it to each other to fall back into our old roles. But despite Grant's absence things were different. We had lost the ability to talk to each other. The clever banter of the Cynthia-and-Michelle Show had no purpose without the audience that school provided. And I—because of Grant? because of your breasts, or your hair that had deepened to enviable rusty red?—I no longer wanted to confide my hopes and dreams. I wanted to be alone.

I wanted to read poetry. I wanted to write poetry. While you had been busy with Grant, I had fallen in love with language and imagination, with the way that Emily Dickinson packed so much meaning into so few words. I wanted to hug her poems close, so close that her brilliance would find its way into my poems. *I taste a liquor never brewed — / From Tankards scooped in Pearl —*

I did not want to share Emily. And I definitely didn't want to share my own poems with you. I was embarrassed, wary of your judgment, uncomfortable with the feelings that poured into my poems at the same time as I gloried in their emotional release. So, like Emily, I locked my fragile poems in a drawer and loved them in secret.

Nor did I want to hear about you and Grant, because every time you brought up his name your voice took on a smugness that grated. When you said his name the cadence and tone of your voice defined you as a woman, a woman of knowledge and experience. You made me feel too young, too stupid, too gawky, too plain me.

At home, Max—age seventeen, two all-important years older than me—used a different brand of smugness, but it had the same effect. He decided he was now one of the grownups, a category from which I was obviously excluded. So every night at dinner—did my mother really serve nothing but liver and onions?—the parents and Max would argue about President Kennedy in Berlin or Martin Luther King and his plan for a March on Washington. As far as I could tell, they mostly agreed with each other, but they said things in different ways and they interrupted and talked over each other. They hardly ever listened. Unless saying 'yes, but . . . ' qualifies as listening.

They ignored me as I cut yet another piece of liver into small pieces and hid it under yet another heaping lump of mashed potatoes. We always have liver but we don't ever live, I thought. Could that be the start of a poem? No. I knew it was just boredom talking in my head.

Years later—I think when Joy was a baby and just starting to eat solid foods—I asked my mother why she had always served liver for dinner.

She turned and gave me a startled look. I can still see her waving the spoonful of baby food fruitlessly in the air, far from Joy's mouth, and hear the surprise in her voice. "But we hardly ever had liver— maybe once or twice a month. I wanted to make sure you got enough iron—and it helped stretch the budget. But I knew you didn't like it. Which is what I told your father when he asked why we couldn't have it more often."

My mother was already dead when I discovered the decadent pleasure of fois gras—its silken texture, unctuous richness, and the residual flavor of lingering guilt—past guilt for hating my mother's liver and present and future guilt for enjoying fois gras so much, knowing what's involved in making it taste so good. I remember a New Year's Eve party where Alex and I put little labels next to each plate of food. Low fat. No nuts. No dairy. Gluten-free. Spicy. The fois gras label said 'only one goose was tortured to produce this morsel.'

Back at the dinner table, where I balefully eyed my tough, oniony slab of liver, I heard Max say, "A bunch of us are going to take the bus to Washington—we think we should be part of the March." I perked up. This would be interesting.

"Nobody's going to Washington," said both parents in unison.

"It's a march for Negroes," my father added.

"Oh, Dad—nobody calls them Negroes anymore—they want to be called blacks, and they get to decide—everybody knows that." Max rolled his eyes. "And the March isn't just for blacks, it's for freedom and jobs. If all kinds of people show up, we'll be harder for the government to ignore."

"You're not going."

"Why not? You don't even have a reason. You're always preaching at us about being responsible citizens, and the first time I actually want to do something the only thing you can say is no. Well, I'm going anyhow." I could feel Max's exasperation in every word.

It turned into a classic family fight. Tempers frayed. All the usual 'you never' and 'you always' accusations received air time. I just watched.

In the end, after my mother convinced my father that he should drive Max and his friends to Washington so that he could keep an eye on them, I announced that I wanted to go too. But I was too late. They had compromised as much as they were going to for one day.

"It's bad enough that Max insists on going. This March is no place for a fifteen-year-old girl. And that's that." As usual, my father had the final word.

I moped and complained, hoping they would give in and take me along. I wanted to go, of course, and I believed that everyone should be equal, but it was the trip itself that I wanted most—the thrill of being in a real city. After they left without me, I listened by myself to Bob Dylan singing *Blowin' in the Wind*—I loved singing the words and imagining that better answers were destined to arrive on the next big wind. That I would eventually get to do something that would make the world a better place. My mother and I watched the March on television and over dinner we talked about Martin Luther King's speech and why it was so good. I felt like I might actually become a grownup soon.

But the March on Washington and even Bod Dylan happened on the far fringes of my all-important inner life. The country and the world seemed to be going well, moving in the right direction—my involvement wasn't wanted, let alone required. So I spent the last few weeks of summer with Emily's poems, internalizing her eloquent, cryptic dashes. What you did with your time I never knew, but I suspect you weren't working for a better world either.

School again. Grant came back, taller than when he left—I now had to tilt my head to look into his blue eyes. He was also the new editor of the school newspaper. And, when I dared to submit one of my summer poems, he printed it on page two of the second issue.

```
A Rhythm, A Tick

(breakfast — —
school — — —
— lunch —
— — school — —
— —
dinner
— — —)


TIMES
183

TIMES
twelve

EQUALS
graduation
```

He stopped me in the hall the next day. "Cool poem."

"Thanks." His blue eyes looked more intense than I remembered. I blushed.

"You should submit more. Seriously."

Was he saying that because I was blushing? I felt myself getting redder. I couldn't tell him that all my other poems were about lost love and agony and death.

"Okay," I said, but only because I needed to get away. I didn't mean it. I should never have submitted any poem, ever. My face became a fire hydrant. "I have to get to class." I still remember how dumb I felt when I said that.

The next day, there he was again. "I mean it, you know. I like your poem. You have talent."

The day after that, he was right behind me in the cafeteria line and he followed me to an empty table. "You're the only person I know who can write a decent poem."

Before I could say anything—before I could even think about turning red—you sat down next to him. He did not look at you—only at your hand on his arm, which he eyed with what looked to me like distaste. Was it possible? Had you had a fight? A funny feeling gathered in my chest.

"What are you two cooking up? Is it a surprise?" You had that smug smile, the one that told me I was hopelessly innocent.

"I'm trying to convince Michelle to submit more of her poems. She's the only one who's not writing about broken hearts and loneliness."

I thought of my drawer filled with lonely poems and blushed on their behalf. I was a fraud. I would never submit another poem.

But I did. "Just something I dashed off," I told Grant when I handed him a new cryptic poem, full of wordplay and dashes. I was so gratified when he laughed. My Emily Dickinson phase blossomed. Even the poems I never showed him were written for him.

You, of course, didn't like any of it one bit. You struck back with your own brand of wordplay. Mitch the Bitch. The reason I hate nicknames to this day. The reason I named my own daughter Joy. Because it couldn't be twisted into anything else—no saccharine diminutive, no nasty rhyming insult.

Other kids loved calling me Mitch the Bitch. I had revealed myself as a weird writer of weird poems. I was vulnerable—they had to tease me. You preened with success every time you heard anyone say it. The only thing that made me happy was that Grant didn't dance with you anymore. He didn't dance with anyone.

Eventually, the less mean kids shortened my new name to Mitch, and that stayed with me through the rest of high school. Mitch, a name that got in the way of Grant becoming anything more than a friend. Mitch, a constant reminder that my breasts stayed stubbornly small, that I was less than a woman, that I had nothing to flaunt except some weird poems that only Grant and I liked.

But time changes everything. Ten years later, when I was pregnant and my breasts grew bigger on a flood of hormones, I discovered how uncomfortable they could be. I was relieved when Joy no longer needed them and they returned to normal—I could run without painful jiggling, I could sleep on my stomach, my body fit into a shape I understood. I forgot about what a mortification my small breasts had been in high school. And now, all these years later, I've come full circle. I look at your picture, with your sagging jowls exposed, and I imagine your large naked breasts, hanging down from your chest like a couple of extra-large jowls. The image makes me laugh. And then I feel sorry for you. No matter how old I get, my nipples will never graze my belly button. Okay, I'm exaggerating, but still—it's a funny image, don't you think? No, it's not. It's mean and bitchy. *What's in a name?*

Despite the teasing, my tight, dash-filled poems made me happy. They made me feel special, they seemed to confirm that I had a way of seeing and describing the world that no one else did, that I had a gift for words, however unappreciated.

But the nickname caused me endless adolescent pain. I wrote different—and very bad—poems in my victimized moods, and like my lonely poems from the summer, they were as awful as being called Mitch the Bitch. Fraud? Poet? Fraudulent poet? Schizophrenic outcast underdeveloped deluded fraudulent pretender poet? That seemed to capture it.

Meanwhile, as I said, President Kennedy got shot. With his death, all pretence to statesmanship and culture vanished from the White House. A crude political hack from Texas took over. Things were getting worse, and not just in high school. Only the Beatles provided any consolation, singing directly to me, declaring that they wanted to hold my hand. Nobody else did.

Senior year was easier. We knew we would escape soon. We focused on the future. On college. On the chance to reinvent ourselves. You and I even became friends again, talking about which colleges we liked best. It probably helped that Grant was off at Harvard.

You chose to go to Berkeley. At Christmas your grandparents explained your absence by saying that it was too expensive for you to come home for a visit. The next summer they reported that you were taking a year off to work so that you could qualify for in-state tuition rates. By the time you graduated with a degree in political science they were too frail to make the trip, but they said they were proud of you.

I chose the University of Pennsylvania, because it was in a city, albeit a dilapidated one—and because, once Columbia turned me down, it was as close as I could get to New York, where I really wanted to live. When I got there I reclaimed my name—I was Michelle again. And when a year or so later the Beatles sang *Michelle, Ma Belle* my world felt, at least for the moment, perfect. I majored in English, despite my parents' opposition.

"You'll never get a good job with just an English degree," they said, probably in unison.

"It's a waste of good money," said my father.

"I'm not going to college just to get a good job—I'm going because I want a good education." I probably flounced out of the room. There was no way I would give up an opportunity to spend four years reading poetry and novels in a romantic collegiate environment in the middle of a real city, in Philadelphia, a city that everyone knew of, a city that was the exact opposite of the outskirts of the middle of nowhere.

I imagine them both looking at the receding back of their hopelessly naive daughter with dismay. But although I was naive—they were right about that—I wasn't that naive. I knew enough to keep my dream of becoming a real poet to myself.

Four years later my parents and my brother, claiming to be proud of me, watched as I and hundreds of other students received our diplomas. In between I had learned a lot about poetry and novels, of course, but also a little bit about how the world works, including racism and sexism, a bit more about politics and protest, and about as much about sex as a prude like me could learn. I was quite sure I now had a well-rounded education.

It had been an eventful time. We—you and I, students across the country, the baby boom generation—saw ourselves as agents of change, arbiters of the moral high ground. We were under thirty and we hadn't sold out. At teach-ins and anti-war rallies we protested the Vietnam War. We cheered Martin Luther King, occupant of the highest level of the moral high ground, when he denounced the US as 'the greatest purveyor of violence in the world.' Because Dow Chemical made a deadly defoliant called Agent Orange we forced their recruiters off campus.

But none of it was enough. The war, the destruction, the number of dead kept growing. Body counts for Vietnamese military deaths, body bags for dead American soldiers, official indifference toward Vietnamese civilian deaths, official denial of Cambodian deaths. 1968: The assassination of Martin Luther King. The killing of Robert Kennedy. The election of Richard Nixon. 1969: News of the My Lai massacre. And Neil Armstrong's first step on the moon. 'One giant leap for mankind,' as though that made everything better.

Oh, and before I forget: sadly, the Yankees didn't make it to the World Series that year. The previously hapless New York Mets won in five games.

We made too many wrong mistakes. — *Yogi Berra*

FRIDAY MORNING: New York City

You wake up early, the sun a bright gleam where the curtains are not quite closed, and for one glorious moment you are oblivious to your very public humiliation. You stretch, your hand hits the headboard. You are now fully awake. And a sour oppression wraps its humid arms around you. You're tempted to retreat under the duvet, but you are not the sort of woman who gives in. You are very emphatic about that. Adversity makes you stronger, you remind yourself, it always has, and you will get through this.

Besides, you have to get up and go meet Jack. Jack's an expensive lawyer, but he's good—you know him from a shared stint on a corporate board where he impressed you by staying focused, by not antagonizing people, but nevertheless bringing them around to his point of view. Those are skills you need right now. And when you called him, he sounded pleased. He thanked you for thinking of him and said that at least you weren't bringing him a boring case.

So you make the effort—you put on the coffee, you shower, you dress for success. Then you pick up the newspaper and see your picture and the guilty-until-proven-innocent headline. You know you shouldn't, but you obsess over it—you parse every word in the headline, in the article, wondering what your enemies will make of it. You imagine them gloating over your picture, which makes you look fat, old and guilty. Which you're not. Unless you are. You go back into your bedroom to find a scarf that will help you imagine that you are young and blameless.

Jack's face is impassive while you talk to him. You remember that one of his skills is never to show what he's thinking.

You respond by becoming more emphatic. "I don't understand any of this—I didn't do anything wrong. God knows everyone was happy enough every time I brought in a big donation—and they must know that donations like that don't just happen—that somebody has to go out and get them. That you have to spend time and money." You throw your manicured hands with their red nails in the air, then wonder why you did that. You've been on television long enough to know that it looks weird when someone brings their hands up like that. You shake your head, trying to regain focus, to get control before your emotions spiral away like your hands just did.

Jack decides he needs to manage you. You can see it in the way he squares his shoulders and suppresses a sigh. A part of you shudders in response. Are you really behaving that badly?

"Let's not jump into the middle of this before we get all our ducks in a row, Cynthia. First of all, I need to know the facts—all of them. What happened, when it happened, what directions you got, what other people were doing, who knew what and when they knew it. Emails, minutes of meetings, your calendar, whatever. I'm not assuming that anything in the media is true—except the salmon. But as far as I know, it's still perfectly legal not to like overcooked salmon." He allows himself a chuckle, pleased with his witticism. "As for the indictment, I'll help you fight that—if and when it comes. But let's not decide on a strategy until we know what's what—and what they've got—or think they've got."

You nod, obedient but irritated. You remember someone telling you—who was it? you can't remember names anymore, you can't even remember his face—anyhow, you remember his words: 'You have two choices—you either take your lawyer's advice or you fire him.' You wish you had the luxury of firing Jack, even though you know he's right. You want nothing more than to have all of this go away, for your life to go back to the way it was. You grip your hands so they won't fly out of control again.

I pledge allegiance:
I play a version — Michael Magee

FRIDAY MORNING: Berkeley, California

I indulge myself—a double cappuccino, a bagel with lox and cream cheese and a big bowl of strawberries—and take my breakfast out to the deck. It's a beautiful day here—early enough that the Berkeley Hills are still covered in fog, so for the moment they can't celebrate their superiority over those of us who live on this flat stretch of land that extends to the shore of San Francisco Bay, where the passing BART trains toll the quarter hours for tens of thousands of us as we spend our days trying to get by, or get along, or just get.

The Berkeley Hills, invisible or not, don't matter today. I'm not worried about who or what might claim superiority over me. I'm tickled pink that—at long last—you are getting your comeuppance. And I'm relishing the opportunity to read about it in my warm California sunshine with a fresh, frothy cappuccino in front of me. Life is good. Although I should be appalled at my delight in your downfall. Because I should be better than I am. Which I'm not. Instead, I'm enjoying the fact that I don't have jowls—a tiny accomplishment, if it's a real accomplishment at all, but I savor it together with another bite of my bagel.

The New York Times is even more delicious than my bagel. It turns out that the damning headline over yet another unflattering photo of you is just the start. The writer had so much fun with innuendo that I'm guessing you must have personally offended him at some point. I especially like the way he brought the whole thing down to a scale that an ordinary person could understand: that final anecdote, with you allegedly—allegedly!—complaining about the food choices in business class—how the salmon was too dry, then the beef was too tough—the way you made a point of not sending back the wine, while making it clear that only your good nature prevented you from rejecting that too—how you felt you and your fellow business class passengers deserved something better. And then the author inserts the final zinger—questioning your charging that flight to the Cancer Foundation in the first place.

When Alex comes out with his own bagel and coffee, I talk all about you and your difficulties and why your downfall makes me feel so gleeful.

He doesn't understand. "But that was fifty years ago." He shakes his head. "How can it still matter?"

"Because it does—because she always came out on top—every time. Whatever I managed to do, she did something bigger—she always trampled on other people, took credit whether it was her idea or not—it wasn't just me, she did it to anyone who threatened her climb to the top. The rest of us played by the rules—she never did—and she always got away with it. Until now. So yes, it feels like finally I can say I told you so, you can't get away with it forever."

Alex shakes his head again. "Are you saying you wanted her life—that you wanted to be more like her?"

I notice that the sun has burned away the fog over the Berkeley Hills, although the air still smells fresh and clean from last night's rain. Alex's question hangs like a smudge in that lovely air. It's a complicated question, but I push it away with a simple response. "Would I rather have grown up to be a right-wing fraudster with fake blonde hair? I don't think so," I say. "Alleged fraudster, I should say." I make sure not to mention your jowls. That would make me sound petty and mean.

He laughs, and the smudge fades. We have a second coffee and talk about whether last night's rain did any good, about how warm it is for March, about what to cook for Max and Sarah, who are in town and coming for dinner.

We haven't seen my brother since last year, probably because his second wife has never seemed comfortable with us. She probably knows that we still wonder why Max married her. Maybe she even knows that we're pretty sure that, after Lisa died, he needed someone to look after his meals and his laundry, so he could bury himself in his work and forget everything else. That he needed someone undemanding. And there was Sarah—recently divorced, all soft around the edges compared to Lisa's sharp elbows and caustic tongue, an accommodating woman whose life revolved around lunch with the girls and golf tournaments, which left her plenty of time to keep Max in clean shirts and to have dinner on the table at seven o'clock. Maybe she knew that we felt Max had settled for too little. She probably doesn't know that we wonder if she drinks as much when we aren't around.

Which reminds us both of a recent dinner with friends—a strange, stilted dinner where Alex and I had to work hard to find new topics to talk about, where first the wife and then the husband lost the thread of the conversation, where the first bottle of wine was half empty when we arrived, the next one empty before we sat down to dinner, and the wife went rigid when the husband got up to open a fourth bottle. That was when we both said, "No more for us, thanks, we have to drive"—as though we had dual controls in our car, we joked on the way home—so the cork stayed in the final bottle and we escaped the tension with twin sighs of relief. And now our friends are getting a divorce after almost forty years of marriage. We rehash that evening again, talk about other memorably uncomfortable dinner parties, make smug statements about how lucky we are that we ended our first marriages when we were still young enough to learn from our mistakes.

I smile at Alex. "Should we serve Max and Sarah hash, or rehash, or something totally new and different?" He laughs, and all is good. I don't notice the smudge anymore.

> With liberty and justice for all:
> *wits quivering | and just this | for all* — Michael Magee

The Seventies: Washington, DC and Santa Cruz, CA

After having the whole country between us for four years. I never expected you to show up in my life again. If I thought about you at all, I assumed you would stay in California, maybe head down to Los Angeles to launch a glamorous career. As for me, I was still hoping to live in New York City, although my former dreams of dancing with a sultry Tony and having breakfast at Tiffany's no longer loomed large. Instead I imagined becoming part of the arts scene—the yeasty, exuberant, talented in-group of artists, writers, musicians, photographers, singers and poets that not only defined the unfettered sixties but also pinpointed the center of the creative universe. Somehow, I hoped, I would figure out how to find them and insinuate myself into their lives.

But I ended up in Washington, DC—because I needed a job, a real job, and as far as I could tell, the only half-decent work for women with degrees in English literature was in the nation's capital. Also because no one in New York offered me anything of any sort.

I ended up working for the government, for the *Monthly Labor Review* at the Bureau of Labor Statistics—even more boring than it sounds—where I was wholly occupied with averages and aggregates and regressions to the mean. Every single article we published included the word 'average' at least forty times. It was a metaphor for my life. I wrote a poem about averages that was published in a local magazine. It was the highlight of my first year in Washington.

And then I was rescued—like a damsel in distress, as I always like to say when retelling my story—by a gracious man who had seen my poem, who felt that I had 'a unique combination of verbal and statistical skills that we could use.' He hired me as a research assistant with the brand new National Public Radio. I was going to help take journalism to new heights and by doing so I was going to make the world better. Heady didn't begin to describe how I felt.

I still remember all of us working together on the feature that launched our new service—the feature we put together on the Vietnam War protest march—a compendium of voices and comments that captured and captivated a nation under enormous stress. I remember splicing the tapes, cutting and interweaving the various interviews into a narrative, and when I got to the one where a reporter said, 'today in the nation's capitol, it is a crime to be young and have long hair,' I tossed my long hair in defiance and felt proud to stand up for the anti-war movement, for democracy and for freedom. It was that feature that put National Public Radio on the political map, defining us as the place to go for honest news.

And I was part of it. Okay, not a big part. Research assistants, especially female ones, were essentially gofers. It was our fault if the dregs in the coffee pot burned dry and the air in the little kitchen stank of scorched coffee. But we sometimes earned approval when we proposed a particularly good story idea in the morning meeting. And when we lined up an interview that turned out well we might be rewarded with a compliment. We had seats at the table where things were happening and that made up for having to keep the table supplied with fresh coffee. And the long hours and the low pay.

A year later, you showed up. "Mitch!" you said. "I didn't know you worked here." Although I was pretty sure you did.

"Cindy," I said, to send you a warning about nicknames.

By then I was a full-fledged researcher with slightly more pay, happily spending ever more hours at work. Younger women were now responsible for the coffee pot. I got to come up with more story ideas, do more research, make sure that our experts could talk on the radio without resorting to jargon, and script the questions the interviewer should ask.

I was also in love with Finn, a bearded graduate student at

Georgetown. He said my poems reminded him of Muriel Rukeyser and gave me a copy of *Breaking Open,* her audacious book of poems that astonished me.

> *What if one woman told the truth about her life?*
> *The world would break open.*

Rukeyser was a feminist, a leftist, a poet with Whitman's breadth of vision, a poet whose language seared my heart and mind and skin all at the same time. Finn brought her poems into my life. He compared my poems to hers. He understood. Of course I loved him.

Finn shared the seventies' love of enormous quantities of male hair and what we would later recognize as indescribably bad taste in clothes. He loved to wear knitted polyester shirts that didn't need ironing and bellbottom jeans, also un-ironed. He loved Led Zeppelin and the Grateful Dead. He loved my long hair and the way I looked in a tie-dyed t-shirt and my own bellbottoms. He was a future professor of English literature, my future first husband, our daughter's father, and eventually my ex-husband.

He grumbled about all the time I had to spend at work, which may or may not have been an example of the feminist leanings suggested by his admiration of Rukeyser. "They're not paying you enough for you to stay at work forever." (Okay, that could be feminist, although if it were, surely he would have offered ideas for getting more pay?)

He also said, "Do you always have to talk about work?" (Harder to skew towards feminism.)

Sometimes, to make it up to him, if there was a lull in my day I would write him a poem. He would offer editorial corrections, even when I wrote him a love poem—a foreshadowing of things to come, as it turned out, but at the time I saw it as helpful. A few of the poems he corrected got published in literary journals., which made us both proud. We were on the verge of moving in together.

The Watergate break-in that would eventually sink President Nixon happened that summer, and I think that's why they hired you as the new researcher. My job was to make sure we had enough interviews to fill the schedule every day, concentrating on the rapidly deteriorating war in Vietnam. Your job was to dig deeper into other juicy stories, especially Watergate—to get to the bottom of that murky 'situation,' as we called it until it turned into a full-blown scandal the following summer.

You seemed happy to see me. "Let's grab a beer after work," you said that first day, pushing your sleek auburn hair over your shoulder. "I want to hear all about what you've been doing."

You looked good. It wasn't just your hair. Your waist was small, which made your hips and breasts look their curvy best; you weren't too tall and too thin the way I was. People could still see bone structure in your face—no one could have predicted your future jowls.

I was flattered by your attention, by the fact that you wanted to spend time with me, that our old friendship still mattered to you. As I remember it, the bar was cool and dark, with the smoky beery smell that I associated with real adults. Outside it was hot and muggy, typical DC summer weather, so it wasn't hard to decide on a second beer. It was even easier to agree when you suggested that we might as well have something to eat too.

Of course I knew it bothered Finn when I spent time away from him, especially if I wasn't working. And drinking beer, as far as he was concerned, didn't qualify as work or even work-related. He refused to understand that important conversations could happen in the casual confines of a bar. What he did understand was that I was having fun—and that he wasn't part of it. I wouldn't say it was exactly jealousy, it was more his way of saying I was important to him, but it was still somewhere in the jealousy ballpark.

Anyhow, back in the cool, smoky bar, you shared stories of your time in the anti-war movement at Berkeley, which, according to you, involved a great deal of sex, drugs and rock and roll—told with a roll of the eyes that left me wondering what your part was—whether you were more observer or participant—or a bit of both. But your stories were entertaining and you moved from one to another without me needing to ask many questions. You offered to put me in touch with people who could help with my research. In between you asked about my time at Penn and how I got my job and what I thought about the people at work. It felt like we were best friends again, giggling at the world—our conversation as refreshing as the beer.

You were—and still are, I think, when you want to be—charming. It's an elusive quality, charm, but we all know it when we see it. And when we get to feel it, when we are subjected to the full, direct force of charm, every one of us goes as gooey with delight as a tickled baby. More, please.

That summer you managed to charm just about everyone at NPR—a tough group much admired for their critical thinking—especially the men who made the decisions. They looked forward to having you in their meetings, they listened when you talked, your jokes made them laugh. You were smart. You quickly developed connections that mattered. With you they got a package deal—sizzle and steak, all in one. You made the rest of us look pale and uninteresting as you absorbed more and more of the spotlight.

Brown was your biggest catch. He was supposed to be mine. A charismatic political activist with only one name, he worked for Congresswoman Barbara Jordan and would later provide you with the inside story as the forces of history moved toward impeaching the President. Do you even remember that I introduced the two of you? No, no one else did either—you got all the credit.

Again we were in a bar after work, drinking beer and talking politics with four or five other staffers in the big round booth we thought of as NPR satellite territory—probably a Friday, celebrating the end of a good week, something we often did. Brown came over to say hi to me. "Cynthia, this is Brown — he's the best guy in Washington for anything about civil rights and Black Power." I introduced the rest of the group to him too, thinking to impress them with the fact that I knew him, but it was you who caught his attention.

I tried to stay in the conversation by talking about Brown's boss, the amazing Barbara Jordan who is still one of my heroes—the first black woman Texas elected to Congress—member of the House Judiciary Committee—friend of Lyndon Johnson. You ignored me, focused exclusively on Brown. He was more polite, but it didn't matter. I was only a work connection, whereas you—well, you had turned on that irresistible charm, and you would matter much more to him. I saw you stroke his arm as he left our booth. I saw him smile.

Brown had one of those smiles with layers of meaning—it was beautiful, it lit up his face, and it came with an ironic afterglow that flirted with mockery. Like his name, which matched his skin. Brown, such a modest name, so unassuming a color, neither as definite as black nor as boring as beige. Just warmth and mystery, a quiet presence. Brown refused to say whether it was his first or last name, whether it was his real name or an assumed one. If someone called him Mr. Brown he said 'my name is Brown,' and waited in silence until the person acknowledged the correction. Then, with a hint of that beautiful mocking smile he would continue the conversation.

You and Brown became lovers. The two of you exemplified an edgy liberal cool; seeing you together reminded me of you and Grant back in high school, only more worldly. The one time the four of us had dinner together, Finn reacted poorly to the coolness and the layered smile and took an instant dislike to both of you. And it was pretty clear too that neither of you thought much of Finn and his garish polyester shirt. As I introduced you I could already see you exchange looks of relief that we were in a cheap ethnic restaurant, a place where you wouldn't run into any people who mattered. You looked still more relieved when the meal was over. The two of you both reached for the check before the waiter could put it on the table, and both said 'I've got this,' so that you could pay and get away from us.

We spent less time together after that dinner. At work your attention was devoted to people who had far more power and influence than I did. After work, Finn expected me to be home, and you and Brown had other commitments, so we hardly saw each other at all. By the following summer, when the explosive revelations around Nixon's secret White House tapes surfaced just as the army was orchestrating America's final, humiliating withdrawal from Vietnam, we were both far too busy to be friends—if we talked to each other at all, it was over a beer on an occasional Friday night, but even then we mostly talked with other people.

It's only now, seeing your face again after all those years, that I fully appreciate the extent to which you and Brown were both using each other. I'm guessing that you also liked each other well enough—after all, you were both young and good-looking and witty—but what mattered was that together you were more powerful than either of you could have been on your own. You were such an attractive couple—at least you were attractive to people on the political left—

and you gave people an opportunity to prove their liberality by inviting you into their homes. *Guess Who's Coming for Dinner,* live and in color, right in their own dining rooms, only easier and much more pleasant.

Brown gave you privileged access to parts of the Watergate story that made your name in media circles. And you gave Brown—and Barbara Jordan's point of view—air time on NPR's unimpeachable platform. Plus, as a couple you gave each other all those informal connections that you have benefitted from ever since. Of course, that kind of relationship lasts only as long as the circumstances that sustain it. After Watergate, when your career paths went in their separate directions, your love affair ended—probably without any hard feelings on either side, although I have no way of knowing.

Neither Finn nor I ever said anything to each other about that awful dinner with you and Brown. We didn't turn your coolness or your haste to get away from us into a shared joke the way we would have earlier. Instead we kept our sense of hurt or insult to ourselves, which should have been a sign that our relationship had already moved beyond its best-before date.

There were other things about Finn I remained oblivious to, although I shouldn't have. Like the way he started belittling my work, assuming that it was something that filled a temporary void in my life—that it would be replaced by marriage and children. The way the cleaning and the cooking became my responsibility. Or his fading interest in my poems.

I ignored all these things because Finn was busy completing his thesis and at the same time trying to distinguish himself by publishing a scholarly article or two, which he was sure would help him in his applications for teaching positions. He spent a lot of time polishing his C.V. and drafting heartfelt cover letters to every college and university in the country that was looking for someone to teach English literature.

Somehow, maybe because I was busy or more likely because I was blind to the obvious, I never put it all together. I failed to grasp that his vision of our future had a 1950s quality: he would be a professor, we would get married, have children and live happily ever after in a large house on a tree-lined collegiate street with me as the full-time mother and housekeeper. And that it would make me miserable.

Instead I focused on what was good between us. Sex, of course. And Finn was the funniest man I ever met—he could recite Monty Python's entire Dead Parrot sketch and Gerard Hoffnung's Bricklayer's Lament word-for-word, including the British accents and the pregnant pauses that were as funny as the words that followed. He made me laugh. Every day. He encouraged me to write poems, even after he no longer bothered to actually read any of them. He talked the talk about feminism.

And then, in the spring of 1974, just as the Watergate scandal was dredging deep, ugly divisions in American public life, I discovered I was pregnant. Finn got down on his knee and proposed on the spot. Then he was offered a teaching job in Santa Cruz. I was dizzy with all the changes, all the hormones. With my impending motherhood any usefulness I had at work—or at least any longterm prospects—went down the toilet like my morning sickness. Finn and I chose a couple of plain gold rings. I found a gauzy dress that floated around my expanding belly. He shaved off his beard, leaving a luxuriant moustache and sideburns, and wore a new pale blue leisure suit with bellbottom trousers. On the way to City Hall we picked a bouquet of cherry blossoms from the trees lining the Mall, laughing at our petty crime. The next day we set off across the country in our old VW Beetle, visiting our parents to tell them the news. We celebrated the final night of our honeymoon with a cocktail at the Top of the Mark in San Francisco and then moved into a small apartment on the outskirts of Santa Cruz, near the university.

What can I say about Santa Cruz? I still have such mixed feelings about the place. It seems wrong that such a pretty town should have caused me such despair. But I didn't want to be pregnant, I didn't want to be unemployed and unemployable, I didn't want to be seventy-five miles from the nearest big city.

On the ninth of August, sitting on our second-hand couch in front of the television watching Nixon resign to avoid impeachment, I couldn't stop myself from crying. I wanted so badly to be back in Washington, back at NPR, an insider instead of an outsider, drinking beer with you and the rest of the gang, sharing the gossip that we couldn't put on the air, thin and comfortable in my own body, not sharing it with an interloper who kicked me and made my back hurt. And I couldn't explain any of it to Finn, jubilant Finn, who was delighted to see Nixon dragged from office, Finn, who had a brand new Ph.D. and the job of his dreams in a pretty college town on the edge of the Pacific, Finn, who wasn't pregnant and never would be. Baffled Finn, who looked at me and said, "What's your problem?"

It got better. I stopped crying. I gave birth to a baby girl, and when I told Finn I wanted to name her Joy, he said it was the perfect name for our beautiful daughter. Fatherhood diluted his ability to detect irony, which I found inordinately pleasing.

As I think back to that time, what strikes me is how clearly the patterns of your future life and mine were laid down in those few years. Yours has the better story arc, although one could also look at it as nothing more than a time-worn cliché: you were in the right place at the right time. You achieved the trademark American Dream (liberated white woman model)—fame and fortune—by exposing the appalling details of Tricky Dicky Nixon's crimes for all the country to see—and by doing it well. And now you find yourself, forty years later, the juicy target of a new generation of young journalists, all hoping to dig up enough dirt on you to achieve for themselves the kind of fame that made Cynthia Lord a household name. Do you ever give any thought to the irony of it?

I do. I love the irony; it's delicious. I let it roll around in my mouth, lingering on my tastebuds, savoring the rich umami substance of it.

I did not feel that way in 1974, when I became the wife and mother part of Finn's American Dream (traditional white male model). While Finn and I were moving to California and bringing our baby into the world, you stuck around NPR just long enough to cover the new President giving Nixon a pardon for any crimes he had 'committed or may have committed' during his time in office—and the national arguments that raged in the aftermath. Then, when Joy arrived you sent me a fragile, cobwebby receiving blanket together with a chatty note saying that you had decided to move on—that you would be working as a researcher on the *Today Show* in New York City—that you were looking forward to working with another Barbara—you were counting on Barbara Walters becoming as important in your life as Barbara Jordan—and that you had been promised some on-air time—I can still see your three exclamation points—probably on the local NBC news station. I was, to introduce yet another cliché, green with envy. It tasted like morning sickness.

After that I lost track of you. I measured out my life in feedings, diapers and the long walks that Joy demanded in exchange for falling asleep. I grew to love those walks—they made up for all the unrelenting drudgery and boredom and exhaustion of childcare and housework. Those walks were my time—time when I was free to think of wordplay and images, line breaks and metaphors or anything at all, for as long as Joy slept and I could push her carriage. 'I had to walk for hours,' I told Finn when I needed to explain why the apartment was messy or why dinner wasn't ready. And if the evening turned out well, despite the messiness and the makeshift dinner, I might show him a poem I had worked on while I was walking.

But some poems, my most important poems, I hugged close and didn't share with Finn. I wrote—and then carefully hid away—a whole cycle of poems that I called *The Bureau of Labor Statistics*. The poems, like alternating current, flipped back and forth between my new job as a mother—about pregnancy and labor and the experience of giving birth to a new little statistic, about things one finds in bureaus—and my old job at the real Bureau of Labor Statistics, where I invented new meanings for concepts like regression to the mean to save myself from drowning in all those averages.

Regression to the Mean

Could mean —
　　　　how kindness vanishes under stress
Might mean —
　　　　halfway there —
　　　　why we never arrive
　　　　at better
Never means —
　　　　repression of the Mean
　　　　aggression toward the Mean
In short —

regression to the mean
means —
everything
trends toward the average
Mean — is normal.

Years later—after Finn and I were long finished—a small publisher in San Francisco brought those poems out as a small chapbook with a line drawing of a very pregnant woman on the cover. And a few people bought it, and maybe read it, before it vanished without a ripple and the world moved on. Nevertheless, I'm still proud of that little book. I think of it as evidence that I knew even then that my life's arc would lack the upward trajectory of yours. Mine was more circular, it always regressed to the mean, never achieved launch velocity. I gave the book to Joy when she was pregnant with Maggie. With a laugh she called it a labor of love and tucked it into a bookshelf.

By the time Joy was a few months old, Finn started accusing me of having lost my sense of humor. Then he would add helpful things like, 'You're not the girl I married'—a statement that irritated me both with its blatant obviousness and its use of the word 'girl.'

If someone said that to me now I would simply say 'Duh' or 'Whatever'—those wonderfully concise expressions of contempt—either one would have been the perfect response. But of course I wasn't perfect. ('Duh,' I can imagine Finn saying, if he were reading this.)

Instead, when he voiced his banal judgments of me, I said things like, 'Was that supposed to be funny?' or 'How could that have happened?'—both of which rank right up there as banal statements too.

I can now see that we were both just tired and irritable from living with a baby in a small apartment that was always cluttered with baby things and books and clothes that weren't put away and garbage that needed to be taken out, far away from relatives and without any close friends who might have helped or at least distracted us from our misery. It's clear in retrospect that we didn't really know each other—we lacked a long enough history together, we didn't know the right words to make things better.

Instead we had something much more damaging—we had Great Expectations of what a wife should be, of what a husband should be, and we both came up short far too often during Joy's first few years. We probably even had Great Expectations about what a baby should be, but she was spared the brunt of our frustrations because, at some deep, probably genetic level, we loved her so completely. Or because she was so much more perfect than we were.

We also had good moments. Like when we named her favorite stuffed animal—a giraffe with a long, floppy neck—Pride, for the pleasure of saying at some point each evening that Pride and Joy were sound asleep. Or the time we shared a bottle of wine after learning that the Santa Cruz soccer team had decided to call themselves the Banana Slugs—sending the university administration into paroxysms of dismay. We slugged back a bottle of plonk to toast the Slugs, and then we opened another bottle to extend the pleasure. If I leave out the horrible headache I had the next day, that's one of my favorite memories of our marriage. As is that perfect day at the beach with gulls and sea lions and surfers and Joy's wonder at the variety of living things—a day that didn't end in tears or arguments, but just flowed from delight to pleasure to stories at bedtime.

We bought a house with a bigger kitchen for me and a study for Finn. The extra space helped. Our clutter was spread out and less noticeable—although it also had room to grow, which became a problem over time. We found new friends, people like us who had babies and young children and mortgages. Having friends made a difference too—they provided a pleasant distraction that we needed.

Christmas morning in our new home, with friends coming for a big turkey dinner. A simple holiday, we'd agreed, because it had been an expensive year—one small gift for each other, a few toys for Joy, plus a vacuum cleaner for the house—and with good food and good friends for a sense of occasion. It felt like a recipe for success.

I can see us still: Finn and I sipping mimosas and eating big apple pancakes with whipped cream. Joy in her highchair playing with her whipped cream, enough of it on her chin to look like Santa Claus.

"Would you like to open your present?" I can also hear Finn's eagerness, see his smile.

"Yes, absolutely—but in front of the tree. Let's finish eating first. Then you can make more mimosas while I get Joy cleaned up."

I remember feeling happy, spooning some of the pancake and whipped cream into Joy's mouth, singing *Joy to the World* as I cleaned her up before releasing her to run into the living room, watching as she tore the paper off her first present. I tied the ribbon from the present around her head to make her laugh and enjoyed the way the lights on the tree made both the ribbon and her hair gleam. I remember thinking that maybe I was getting better at the whole housewife and mother thing, that maybe all I had needed was more space and a slightly older child.

Finn asked Joy to bring me the square box with the big red bow. I was puzzled by the shape, by the shift of something heavy inside—I had imagined Finn would give me a book of poetry, something small and thoughtful. "What's this?"

"Open it." That smile again.

"Joy, can you help me take the bow off?" She pulled it and gave it to me. I added it to her hair and she laughed again. "And can you help me with the paper?" The paper fell to the floor. I was holding a box with a border of air holes. It was a Pet Rock.

"Is this supposed to be funny?"

"I thought you'd like it."

The fight continued over a long, boozy turkey dinner, where we each had an audience for our point of view. Finn read parts of the owner's manual aloud, about how easy it was to teach a pet rock to sit or play dead, but how it would always need the owner's help to roll over. I rolled my eyes, without any help. Everyone laughed, either at Finn's reading, which he did with the same dramatic emphasis that he had brought to Monty Python in our good old days, or at me with my exaggerated asides about passive-aggressive Christmas presents. It didn't matter. We had turned into one of those dysfunctional but witty couples—the kind of couple that makes other people feel better about their marriages. As you can see, despite our attempts at improvements, Finn and I continued hurtling along our path toward becoming a divorce statistic.

A Pet Rock—a joke invented in a bar by an advertising man who became a millionaire in the six or eight months before the fad faded—how could Finn have thought that I would want one? Maybe, maybe—to be more generous than I was capable of·at the time—he thought I would appreciate that Pet Rock as a metaphor or a symbol of all the things that were going wrong with America—the disconnect between money and value and meaning, the craving to get rich quick without any effort. He might have thought of it as raw material for a poem, although I didn't need to own something to write a poem about it. No, the truth is that I can't explain his choice now any more than I could then. Except that it was a cheap gift, it was an easy gift, and he didn't care enough to think about something better.

It's odd how something as meaningless as a Pet Rock could lodge so solidly in my memory, while bigger events faded into the background or even disappeared. I'm embarrassed to admit that all that's left in my head about Jimmy Carter's election and his four years as President is a fuzzy memory of him telling us all to wear sweaters instead of turning up the heat in our houses—a more sensible suggestion than he got credit for—and that he was wearing a hopelessly un-cool cardigan to set an example.

That cardigan became a poem. OPEC and the oil crisis became a couple of poems. Stagflation became a snide sonnet on the pride of owning our heavily mortgaged home—with its mortgage fixed at only nine percent—as rates soared and house prices climbed. The Love Canal tragedy grew into a long poem that started in the 1920s when the abandoned canal was turned into a chemical waste dump—and ended with birth defects and cancer and the destruction of what was intended as a model community, the residents sent away so we could forget them, along with all the other abandoned toxic waste sites and their nameless victims. And then I filed my poems away and forgot both them and the events that inspired them, because a marriage headed toward divorce absorbs a lot of time and energy.

I did not write any poems about you. You had not yet become a high-profile on-air journalist and I wasn't thinking about you. But while my life continued in its prosaic cycle of mothering, shopping, cooking, cleaning and fighting with Finn, with the occasional guilt-filled time off to work on my poems, you were making crucial connections and building your career.

When I read your autobiography many years later, I learned that it was you who convinced your bosses at the *Today Show* that Margaret Thatcher was going to be a force in the world, and that you took it upon yourself to befriend her, to earn her trust. According to your version, you were the one who got her to agree to that interview with Barbara Walters, and then you were instrumental in making sure that Thatcher would have the opportunity to lay out her agenda for smaller government and lower taxes. You prepared the research so that Walters would ask tough questions, but none that would make Thatcher sound defensive. Even when Walters quoted a critic who called Thatcher 'ruthless and ambitious, an iron butterfly,' Thatcher took it as a compliment. Best of all—because all three of you understood the synergies between good television and good politics—you persuaded Thatcher to announce to that huge American audience that she would be the Prime Minister of Great Britain within four years.

In 1979, when that prediction came true and Margaret Thatcher took over as Prime Minister of Great Britain, you and your career took a steep turn, upwards and to the right. From that point on, the people who mattered to you were largely white and right. You reflected the change in America and Britain faster and better than almost everyone and you employed the new political vocabulary with consummate assurance. The only remaining link to your youthful sixties and seventies—to the team at NPR and to Brown—was that almost all the important people around you were still male. But as far as I could tell, you never gave your past a passing thought.

As for me, nothing in my life in the seventies went up or to the right. I realize, as I reread my poems from those years, that almost everything I wrote back then was dreary or cynical or—at their very worst—both. The promise of the sixties, the joy of the Beatles, my youthful dreams—all gone. But the way I remember it, I wasn't alone. It seems as though everyone in the whole country—except you and a very few others—was miserable in the seventies, as if the rest of us already knew that things would only get worse. My poor poems were my consolation—my excuse for not doing anything real, anything meaningful, for being too busy looking after Joy and Finn to get involved, for only complaining to friends who already agreed with me.

My other consolation was the New York Yankees. Living in

California I had to keep my partisanship a secret, of course, but I exulted that day that Reggie Jackson hit those three home runs in the final game of the World Series against the Los Angeles Dodgers. And then again the next year, when they beat the Dodgers once more for their second World Series title in a row. But even baseball had changed for the worse—by the end of the seventies the owners were all greedy bastards, the best players were all grasping millionaires and it felt like money was ruining baseball the way it seemed to be ruining everything else.

When you come to a fork in the road, take it. — *Yogi Berra*

LATER FRIDAY MORNING: New York City

You clutch your hands firmly in your lap, aware that they still want to fly up and away. You yourself would like to follow them to wherever they want to go. Instead you sit straight, careful not to slump back in your chair, and you make the effort to force your shoulders down. You breathe.

And then your expensively competent lawyer says the word you've been dreading.

You can't help yourself. You lean forward and your left hand strikes his desk. "How can they say it's fraud? I've never done anything—I was doing my best to help them raise money—you have to spend money to make money—everybody knows that. How serious is this?" A toss of your blonde hair, a glint of tears of rage, a blink to clear them. Then you withdraw your hand, get it back under control, your right hand clutches your left and drags it back into your lap.

Jack gives a half shrug and leans back into his chair, which tilts as if to help him remove himself from your outburst. "It's serious, Cynthia—I don't want to mislead you. They're already talking about an indictment. Now tell me what happened. Take your time." He gives you another nod to encourage you.

You breathe deeply and lean your body back in your own chair, which doesn't have a tilting mechanism. You decide not to care anymore what your hands want to do. You start. You tell Jack about being asked to join the Cancer Foundation board, about the celebrity welcome they give you. Then you tell him how you learn about the annual rare wines auction, how a senior board member explains to you that your job is to help bid the price of the wines up and up. How when your bid wins, you pay up, take the bottle home and put it away until next year, how you donate it back to the Foundation for the next auction—in return for a big charitable receipt. It's a simple win-win for everyone, you tell Jack—your red fingernails emphasize the point—more money for the Foundation, bigger charitable receipts to the donors. Everyone knows that no one will ever open the wine and drink it—it's likely been vinegar for years already but no one talks about that, that's not the point—and that every year the bottle gets older and the charitable receipt gets bigger. You find that the telling helps you feel calmer—you are, after all, a professional communicator, you know how to frame a story, you know how important it is to demonstrate that you did nothing out of the ordinary, nothing that everyone else wasn't doing.

Jack is a good lawyer. He listens, nods, occasionally leans forward to jot a note on his legal pad. You sense that he is a man who understands everything—and a man who judges nothing.

Next you tell him about the invitation to join the board of the medical devices manufacturer—the first woman on their board, you say, with a trace of pride that you are probably no longer entitled to—and then how the pharmaceuticals firm recruited you as well. How you encouraged both companies to increase their charitable donations, not just to the Cancer Foundation but to other charities as well. How both companies chose to give GIKs—gifts-in-kind—because, they told you, it was more cost-effective. You emphasize to Jack that you never knew the details—that even if they did get receipts for many times the value of their donations—which hasn't been proved and might never be proved—that you had nothing to do with how they went about setting a value for their donations. "I never claimed to be an accountant," you say with a touch of exasperation, raising your hands, palms up, in classic denial.

"Okay, good," says Jack when you come to the end of your tale. "We can review all of this once you get your documentation together. Assuming it all supports your story, I can't see this going to trial." He makes another note on his pad. "One question: you billed the Cancer Foundation for your airline tickets?"

"That was a mistake — my assistant handles all of that and I never checked what she did."

"But you signed the expense claims?"

"Probably—I sign lots of stuff—I don't remember." You manage a smile that you hope looks natural. "You know how it is—I'm always busy—I depend on my people to do their jobs right."

"Okay—we should probably stop there for today. Do I need to tell you not to talk to the press about any of this?" His faint smile reminds you of Brown. You are disconcerted and fail to reply.

But he is already asking his final question. "One last thing—is there anything else I should know?"

You deny the existence of anything more by giving him your most charming smile. It feels almost natural. You again force your shoulders down as you stand up, you free your hands so that you can shake his. You thank him for his time and then you check that your scarf is in place before leaving his office. How much does he believe, you wonder, as the door closes behind you.

> I pledge allegiance:
> *I pay a lawyer — Michael Magee*

LATER FRIDAY MORNING: Berkeley, CA

As I push my cart through the crowds at the Monterey Market I think of Allan Ginsberg: *Aisles / full of husbands! Wives in the avocados, babies in the tomatoes!* —although there aren't many husbands here, mostly wives and babies, and the tomatoes still look like cardboard this early in the season. But I could make a salad with avocados and grapefruit—plus some watercress. And some pasta with fresh crab and asparagus. Sarah is a vegetarian—why did Max marry her?—but she still eats seafood once in a while, and Max will definitely enjoy it. If the warmth holds, we can eat out on the deck.

Distracted by Ginsberg and dinner, I nearly collide with Ardith, my favorite friend, a poet who still dyes her hair red and wears bright scarves with more flair than you do, a woman who has never suffered fools at all, let alone gladly. The perfect person to listen to my stories about you. I give her a hug. "Coffee?"

Up the street at a tiny cafe we settle in for a comfortable talk— weather, food, news of the day, poetry. Ardith is a talker—even the weather is interesting when she talks about it. The conversation flows. Somehow we find ourselves wringing our hands over the unsolvable crises unfolding in the Ukraine and Syria and Nigeria. And the longer term conundrum of global warming. To rescue us from the gloom, I take charge. "But there is some good news," I tell her. "Cynthia Lord is being indicted for fraud. You remember that I grew up with her, and that we worked together way back at NPR?"

Ardith's face is a picture of eager delight. She loves good gossip as much as I do. "So—tell me the full story—I want the inside scoop—what was she like?"

I tell her about your start in the Berkeley Free Speech movement, back when being young and liberal was the last word in cool. Then about NPR and Brown and how you played the power and influence game. How we went our separate ways, me to motherhood and you to the *Today Show* and fame and fortune. How you became the biggest sell-out I've ever known personally. I remind her of what happened at my book launch. How much I'm enjoying your fifteen minutes of shame. "But what I really don't understand is why she would risk everything—just to save a few dollars on charitable donations and airplane tickets. It doesn't make sense."

Ardith looks at me and raises an eyebrow. "Come on—that's exactly how rich people get rich and stay rich—they always get other people to pay—apparently even for their charitable donations—so they can keep more for themselves. Behind every rich person there's a trail of frauds or people who have been badly used—or both. And every once in a while—like now, maybe—they get caught out. So— do you think she's actually going to go to jail?"

"It's hard to tell—all I'm sure of is that she'll get herself a good lawyer."

"And probably get somebody else to pay for him too."

I drink the rest of my coffee. "Alex thinks I'm enjoying all this far more than I should—that I'm being petty and mean. And maybe he's right."

"Why shouldn't you enjoy yourself? Ignore Alex—if you're mean so is most of the country—I imagine everybody's talking about it. That's why those articles are on the front page. And Cynthia Lord is public property whether she likes it or not."

Ardith seems so sure of what she's saying. I can't tell whether I'm jealous or reassured by her certainty. "Sometimes life imitates poetry," she says, and then quotes Longfellow. *"Though the mills of God grind slowly / Yet they grind exceeding small.* Don't you love it when poetry becomes relevant?"

"Poetry's always relevant," I say, trying to match her certainty. "The problem is that mostly no one realizes it." She laughs, and we hug goodbye.

I watch her as she walks away, as she straightens her posture against the creak of arthritis in her hips and knees, and adjusts her scarf for maximum appeal. Ardith has sparked an idea I should have thought of already—I need to turn your downfall and my unquenchable glee into poetry. It may be the only way to find the answer to Alex's question, which is still a grey niggle at the edge of my mind. But I already know that, unlike Longfellow, my poem won't leave retribution to God.

> With liberty and justice for all:
> *will ever try* / *and just this* / *for all* — *Michael Magee*

The Eighties: Berkeley, CA

Looking back, I'm surprised to see how easily I could label the sixties our Technicolor decade, how it still feels right. The other decades are more elusive, although the fifties, now that I think about it, were our milk-teeth years. The time when we learned to bite, but didn't yet do any damage—when we lost ourselves in play and sometimes forgot to bite—when we were bitten without being hurt.

Then I look at the chaos of the seventies, the way we swerved and flipped through those slippery years, and I can't see beyond a hopeless tangle of possible themes and symbols, each inadequate in its own way. It's complicated, as we say now when we want to acknowledge complexity without actually dealing with it. But the seventies are behind us. Let's move on.

That's what Finn and I did, after our marriage collapsed. We were both more than ready, so only Joy felt the need to whimper. I told Finn I'd found a teaching job in Berkeley, in the same school where Joy would be enrolled; that Joy could stay with him every second weekend, for a month in the summer, and a week over Christmas; that if I got the equity in our house—the house that harbored all our resentments, we had to get rid of it, which both of us realized, although neither said it out loud—we could go our separate ways without any ongoing financial obligations; that he should keep the car. In a voice that I had learned at NPR, a voice that induces obedient acceptance, I told him it was a fair offer as far as I was concerned. It worked. Or perhaps Finn recognized that he wasn't in a position to negotiate.

He had other priorities. Finn was having an affair with one of his students. He was in love, he said. It was the real thing. She gave his life purpose and meaning. Unlike his wife, who was mean, but no longer had meaning, which he also didn't say but was probably thinking. Joy—six-year-old Joy, one year younger than our granddaughter Maggie is now—was caught in the unavoidable fallout, but I don't think he was thinking about her at all. Maybe I wasn't either.

With the cash from the Santa Cruz house that sold for the asking price, plus some help from my parents and a mortgage from the bank, I bought a tiny, dilapidated bungalow within walking distance of our new school. Joy hated it as soon as she saw it.

"It's so-o-o small," she said when we arrived. "It stinks," she said, as soon as she walked in, with her unassailable six year old judgment. "I hate it," she said, walking out and sitting down on the front steps.

"You'll like it after we fix it up." I tried to blink away the soggy miasma of failure that gathered behind my eyes. I had no idea how I could afford to do more than maybe paint a room or two. "You can choose whatever color you like for your bedroom." Did I sound chirpy? I hated mothers who chirped at their children.

"I don't care," she said. "I'll still hate it." She refused to come back in.

It was the best I could do, I wanted to say. I wanted to justify myself, to get across to her how things had gone so wrong, to explain why this strange old house would be better for me, for us, than the bigger, newer, familiar house in Santa Cruz, to tell her how sorry I was that her parents couldn't stay married. But there was no way to have that conversation with a six year old, much as I longed to plead with her, to be able to convince her that this really was for the best, that she didn't need to be so angry.

Somehow we muddled through the next few days, and then the next few weeks, and then months. A combination of Mr. Clean and fresh air from open windows made the house smell better. Or maybe we just got used to the old house odor. At least I did. In any event, Joy finally stopped complaining about it. I painted her room a vivid turquoise that matched her favourite stuffed cat—although the cat disappeared not long after the room was finished. I discovered that we could walk to the BART station and take the train into the city. I relished those brief moments when I felt I had reclaimed my life, when I felt almost as free and happy as I had before I met Finn.

Except when I didn't. On Finn's weekends, Joy would wait for him to arrive with a look on her face that reminded me of you on that long-ago Saturday when your father never showed up. She was unreachable. After her father drove away with her, I would attack the jobs that were too big to do when she was with me—I scrubbed the old kitchen cabinets or the oven or the aging linoleum floor with a fury, as though it were Finn I was scrubbing of all his hateful habits and tics and acid asides. As though I could scrape away the hurt of rejection or my own stubborn patina of unlovableness. Or restore Joy's innocence.

Eventually the kitchen sparkled, as clean and sweet-smelling as a 1950s commercial. And the bathroom. But I still felt waves of anger—at Finn, at the banality of it all, the awful predictability of our divorce. If Finn could see me now, I thought, the perfect housewife of his dreams. I tried to exhaust my anger during long, fast runs, or vent it by slamming closet doors and cupboard doors. The wind, the motion, the thunk of shoes on pavement, the satisfying tuneless noise of wood hitting wood and glasses rattling—it all helped, at least for a little while, but under the anger was an ulcer that remained raw and sensitive.

And every second Sunday evening, after Finn brought Joy back home, she would bounce off the walls as if they were indefensible boundaries. 'Dad lets me—Dad doesn't make me—Dad always—Dad never—I hate you.' Her barrage would continue, slowly becoming less strident, until by Tuesday it was mostly gone and I had something resembling a cooperative daughter back. It exhausted me. It depressed me. It made me feel guilty. It made me angry at Finn. But I stopped myself from calling him, from insisting that he do things my way so that Joy wouldn't feel so torn, because I knew that he would tell me to give her the same limits that he imposed or didn't, and the freedoms he gave her, and I knew that if I did he would change them, so that I would still and always be wrong.

Looking back, now that I'm too old for that kind of hot anger, I can only wonder at how narrow my perspective was. I can see that Finn too must have been on the receiving end of Joy's confusion and fury, that he was forced to absorb exactly as much acting out, and that he saw a whole lot less of the other Joy—the little girl who needed two days to suppress yet again her angry resentment at being the child of a broken home, forced to wear cheap clothes that she loathed with all her heart.

In the evenings after Joy went to bed, I turned on the television for the noise and distraction of other people. And there you were, back in my life, with your hair newly blonde and bouffant—a rising star at NBC—reporting from the Republican National Convention. It should have been a boring convention, since Ronald Reagan had already won the nomination in the primaries, but you told the unfolding story with all the verve and panache of a spy thriller, keeping me and millions of other Americans from turning off our TV sets. You did it even better with the Democratic convention, where you had better raw material to work with—Ted Kennedy arriving at the convention planning to change the rules so that he could replace President Jimmy Carter as the Democrats' candidate, then encouraging delegates to join him in his contempt toward the incumbent, and finally giving the best speech of his career despite not getting his way. You managed to engross the nation in the drama of political manoeuvres and shifting alliances as they played out in front of us.

You were good. Maybe because I was lonely, or vulnerable, or because it was a long time since we fought for the same prize, I felt proud that I knew you. I wrote you a note congratulating you on your work, telling you how much I was looking forward to watching you on election night. And you took the time to write back, which pleased me even more, a note saying that I should get in touch if I were ever in New York.

By then I was so far removed from journalism that I never once wondered how you unearthed the stories you told us. The story itself—and your skill in telling it—captivated me. Later, when you wrote about the 1980 election in your book, you again glossed over the details. 'It came to my attention,' you wrote, or 'I learned.' I failed to ask the key questions—who were your sources, how did you get your information, and how much of it was true?

Meanwhile, the first day of school was getting closer, bringing with it an amorphous threat of still more upheaval in our lives. Joy and I were both on edge. Her biggest wish was to go back to her school in Santa Cruz. "Why can't we go back? That was a way better school!" Now, as I think back to those difficult days, I recognize—for the first time—how she came to be a Republican. That first enormous change in her life was, from her point of view, entirely negative—all loss, no gain—and she's been wary of change ever since.

In the end, she focused on whether there would be girls in her class. "How can you be sure? You don't know." I remember her stamping her foot in frustration—at the vagueness of my answers, or the unfairness of the situation I had forced on her, or possibly at the irritation in my voice.

In the end, so that we could change the conversation, I resorted to bribery. "Tell you what, Joy. If there are no other girls in your class, I promise you can have all the chocolate you want, every day, until you start second grade."

"And if there are no girls next year either, can I have another year of chocolate?"

"Absolutely." Her smile was pure sunshine.

The next morning, she faked despair when she realized she would probably miss out on a year of chocolate. "What if there's only one other girl? Do I still get all the chocolate I want?"

"Only on Wednesdays."

Yes, I know—bribery is lazy, shoddy parenting—but it worked. After all, bribing my daughter with virtual chocolate—how bad could that be? At least it appeared to ease her anxieties about her new school. It wasn't like it was fraud or breach of duty—nobody was going to indict me.

Maybe it worked for Joy, but I know my own worries were not assuaged with chocolate. Too often I felt like a walking cautionary tale with a sign that said Single Mother strapped to my chest. I worried about Joy and what the divorce was doing to her. I worried that I would fail as a teacher. That my life would always be a lonely struggle with too little money. That I would grow old spending my days lugging bags full of groceries home on the bus, overwhelmed by a life I never intended to live. While watching you soar ever higher into media mecca.

Things started to get better when I met Ardith. Joy and I were in a used bookstore on Telegraph Avenue, one of the cheap places we would go on a Saturday afternoon. And while she searched for the 'one best book' she was allowed to choose in the children's section, I was free to browse in the cramped, dusty poetry section, sometimes for almost half an hour. That day I was looking through a stack of magazines—some carefully bound issues printed on heavy paper, others just photocopied sheets of cheap paper, stapled together—when a woman with red hair and a blue and purple paisley scarf exclaimed with delight and pulled a battered bunch of paper, titled BEZOAR, out of my pile.

"You must read this," she said, holding it out to me, almost pushing it into my hand. "Do you know Ron Silliman? This has a fantastic poem about BART in it—the whole thing—all eight or ten pages—is one long sentence, and it's wonderful." She looked at me as though my response mattered to her.

"Sorry," she said, her eyes flitting from my face to the magazine that I had accepted from her and back again. "I hardly ever see anyone in the poetry section—and then to see you and my favorite Silliman poem all at the same time—it's just perfect. My name's Ardith. Do you come here often?"

We talked about poetry, about how poetry is so much more than words on paper, more than carefully crafted, beautifully organized words on paper. We finished each other's sentences, about poetry as a community of people, some alive, like Silliman, many—like my beloved Emily Dickinson and Ardith's inscrutable Gertrude Stein—dead and gone. We talked about caring about words, about how they sound and how they can mean more than just what they mean, about playing with words to see if they can make better connections—to each other and to other people—people who are thoughtful and care about the things that are important, people who don't use words like 'things' as sloppy placeholders for vague ideas.

When Ardith laughed at my joke I knew I had found a friend.

Bezoar, I later learned, can be either a gastric stone, possibly with magical qualities, or a wild goat, or a hairball. A perfect distillation of Silliman's poem, with its accretion of words that magically reveal an entire city and its inhabitants. I imagined the poet laughing at the idea that he could be the wild goat, at play—or at work—in the Bay Area's guts.

Ardith introduced me to her collection of women who love poetry, some single like her, others divorced, plus a sixty-something widow. And that's how my new life took on a shape outlined by women and poetry, how my despairing sense of eternal failure thinned like fog in the sunshine. We got together most often at my house, because I was the youngest, the only one with a child to look after. The women would arrive with casseroles and salads and cheap wine, and we would talk and read poems and talk some more until it was late and we were giddy with laughter, which was usually when Joy came out to tell us she couldn't sleep and everyone went home.

Although I didn't know it, that was the start of my years without men. I found myself surrounded by women—not just my new friends, but also the teachers I worked with, the mothers in our neighborhood, and most of the people I talked with in stores. Joy, too, surrounded herself with girls—girls who, happily, dominated her first grade class. Her new best friend lived two streets away.

There were, of course, males on the periphery—some of the neighbors were husbands, the man at the fish counter was happy to talk to me about his garden and the weather, there were boys as well as girls in my class, I talked to Finn when he picked Joy up and dropped her off again. But for a very long time I don't think I touched a single man. Except maybe I brushed fingertips with the fish man when he handed me my carefully wrapped fillets. Finn and I definitely never touched. I would leave Joy's suitcase on the doorstep so that I didn't need to hand it to him. And when she came home again I made a show of hugging her, as though she had been away for a very long time, leaving Finn to drop her bag inside the door.

Slowly, I discovered how to enjoy small things again. Or what we would now call balance, or mindfulness, or living in the moment. My low expectations around teaching—I wanted the job mainly because the hours matched Joy's school day—reduced my career disappointment. I learned to find satisfaction in my kids' mastery of new skills. And living alone with Joy revealed freedoms I had forgotten—the freedom to serve pancakes for dinner on Sunday night and eat them in front of the television, or to leave dirty dishes unwashed without starting an argument, to turn on the light in the middle of the night and read in peace, to drink wine with my friends without a disapproving presence whose standards had been violated. Other than Joy, of course.

Poems and revisions of poems cascaded from my fingertips into notebooks that piled up on the tiny desk in my bedroom. Each new notebook felt like it added substance to the idea of me as a poet. And editing the poems, starring the best ones, sharing them with Ardith— that was best of all. She was the perfect reader—she told me what she liked and why she liked it, but she also pointed out lines that didn't quite work and encouraged me to keep fixing them until they did. Watching her read one of my poems, slowly, like it mattered, then watching her think about it and reread it made me feel braver.

And so I sent them out, and although most of them were ignored or rejected, some were published in literary journals with limited circulation. Credibility, Ardith called it, every time one of us published a poem. Recognition. Poets need fans just like baseball teams, she said, winking at me. We celebrated every small success and—more often—commiserated over each rejection. Our motto, our toast: poetry matters.

You and the rest of the country weren't paying any attention to poetry, of course. After all, most people have always found baseball more interesting, and that was a pretty good year for baseball. The Phillies won their first World Series title ever. Even more people, including baseball fans and poets like me and journalists like you, were caught up in the polarization of the nation as the political campaign unfolded. On the Republican side were Ronald Reagan, the Moral Majority, the National Rifle Association, and—fatally, for Carter's chances—optimism. On the other side, President Carter offered nothing except worry—that Reagan was a dangerous right-wing radical, that he was a war hawk, that valuable social programs from the New Deal to the Great Society would be unravelled in pursuit of lower taxes. Carter's honest folksiness was reframed as naive foolishness. His every attack on Reagan boomeranged. Worst of all was his failure to advance a single plan or policy.

And throughout the campaign, every time you uncovered yet another dramatic divide between the two candidates, the two parties, liberal and conservative voters, your glee was palpable. I can still hear Ardith saying, as we watched the panel discussion after the debate, "She looks like she just blew out all the candles on her birthday cake—and she knows her wish will come true."

It was obvious, at least to Ardith and me, that you were on the side of optimism—that you had moved decisively to the right. And why not? When your annual Christmas card arrived that year, with a picture of you and a sexy man on horseback with mountains in the distance, we discovered that you had married your cameraman and that he was devoted to you. So maybe Ardith was wrong—it wasn't a birthday cake or the Republican triumph that explained your exuberance. Not that it mattered. Both you and Ronald Reagan reflected your personal happy expectations for the future—and the promise of your star power—onto the voters. In return, the voters—more than enough to give Reagan a resounding victory—were happy to soak up a little of the gleaming radiance that made the two of you special.

The poets and I understood that the public had been convinced to drink the Kool-Aid and that things would get worse. We ourselves, out of step with the country, read our sad poems or savage poems to each other. And we commiserated with cheap wine—I like to remember it as white wine, so as not to taint us with anything red and Republican, although Republicans didn't own the color yet—and critiqued each others' poems with a small, imperfect kindness.

Learning to celebrate small achievements probably helped me learn to like teaching too. Not that I realized it at the time. In those early years I was still daydreaming about going back to NPR, still wishing that I could live a larger life. But that first year of teaching, within that third grade classroom with my twenty-six students, I could, if I worked hard, foster a community where creativity was encouraged and learning was applauded, where the essence of good citizenship revolved around respect for others. There were days when it didn't work—days when it seemed like every one of my students had invented a new way to frustrate me—but in general, over time, they figured out that kindness worked within our four walls, that they were safe and appreciated.

Your workplace, I suspect, was the complete opposite—big and important, but also much less kind. I imagine NBC offered regular servings of all-American competition and infighting. A version of NPR, but without the justification of honest, accurate journalism as a reason for being—just a struggle for viewers and advertisers, and let the losers fall where they may. This is all hindsight, of course. Back in 1980 I was quite simply awestruck, seeing you, who I had played with and worked with, on national television.

If I had known Alex then, and if he had asked me if I wanted to be you, to live your life, I would have wondered why he bothered to ask. Of course my answer would have been yes. You had the perfect job, an admiring public, plus a man who adored you—although even then I was puzzled that he was a cameraman, not a media mogul or high profile politician. But his muscular sexiness reminded me—just a bit—of Brown. Maybe he had some of Brown's subversive edginess too. I amused myself by nicknaming your husband Pink, to match his complexion. It was snarky enough to make me think that, no, maybe your life wasn't entirely perfect.

But you had it—whatever it is that it takes to succeed. Maybe you still do. You were a fast learner, as I remember it, and worked hard. You figured out how to suck up to the right people, how to maneuver through all the backbiting and phoniness and pretence that one had to be part of. You identified which people you could—no, you had to—step on so that you could get there faster and wow the people in charge.

Already by the time I was leaving NPR, you knew how to get invited to the right dinners and parties. You loved having an excuse to get your nails done and wear a dress that showed off your cleavage—and relished the access it gave you. It was all good for your career—the way you were able to insinuate yourself into rooms full of influential people—the way you learned to stand out in those rooms. Which would explain why, as Ronald Reagan and Margaret Thatcher gained prominence, you replaced your former left-wing sensibility with a new right wing ideology as if your politics were a fashion statement. Follow the power, become like them—that's how to build your own power. And so you took on their color even before it became their color—Republican red, like your fingernails. They adopted you as one of their own. And among other things, they must have introduced you to the career benefits of getting involved with charities.

Meanwhile my life continued along a different path, anchored by Joy, and with Ardith leading the way. At some point she started hinting that I should put a collection of my best poems together. I ignored her. At some later point her hints turned into a demand. She said she knew a man in San Francisco who published poetry, that he would—or at least should—like my poems. After dithering and worrying, I worked on my older poems, on the theory that their rejection would hurt less. The result, painstakingly typed out on Ardith's first personal computer while she babysat Joy and I fretted over every line break, was forty poems.

I could go on forever about the delirious publishing process, from the nerve-wracking submission and the interminable wait to the euphoric yes, from editing to cover design to Joy's big-eyed amazement when I showed her the proof copy with my name on the cover.

"Will we be rich now?" she asked, her small body vibrating with excitement.

Her face fell and her body went slack when I answered no.

"I have homework to do" was all she said, retreating down the hall to her room.

Nevertheless, that little book felt like a distilled confirmation of all the decisions, good and bad, that I had made since I wrote my first poem. The world was good—I was a published poet.

When I wrote to tell you about my book, you sent me a congratulatory letter. You said you had to be in San Francisco and that we should get together. The timing was perfect—you would be here for the launch—at City Lights, the legendary bookstore of the Beat Generation—and we could go out for a late dinner afterwards. You said you'd be there. You said you were looking forward to it, that you couldn't wait to read my poems.

All of us were so excited—Ardith and the poets, my publisher, my parents who made a special trip just for the launch, even the other poet who was sharing the launch with me—but me most of all. A genuine star was going to grace the occasion and turn it into something important and glamorous and extra special. But of course—I should have known—you never showed up and you never looked forward to it and as far as I know you never so much as held a copy of my book.

What you did do was send flowers. It was the biggest, gaudiest flower arrangement I have ever seen, unless you count movie versions of mobster funerals. Stargazer lilies, with their overwhelming scent. Long spears of purple gladiolus and every other flower in every color imaginable. They were delivered late, after we had waited for you, after people had started looking restless, just after the publisher had introduced me and I was on the verge of reading. The huge vase and the top-heavy flowers took up the entire book table. The flowers loomed over the low ceilinged basement space even after the publisher moved them from the book table to a corner, on the floor.

Your flowers dominated everything—me, the other hapless poet, our slim volumes of poetry, the attention of the audience. One of the guests was overcome by the fumes before I had finished reading and apologized on her way out. 'Allergies,' she said, waving a Kleenex. Other people exclaimed over them or consoled me because you weren't there—'but how nice of her to send you flowers,' they said. In smaller groups they gossiped and speculated about you. You sidelined our poems without even bothering to show up. I did not share your tiny note in its tiny envelope: *Sory I cant be their — best Cynthia.* The note was typed.

If you count the copy of *The Bureau of Labor Statistics* that I traded with the other poet, we managed to move twenty-seven copies of my little book that evening. Which the publisher was gracious enough to say was pretty good for poetry. I think my parents bought ten copies, and Ardith bought another five.

I never got in touch with you again after that carefully choreographed humiliation. You continued to send me your Christmas letters, as I'm sure you did to thousands of other people you happened to meet, if only because it was easier to send it to the whole list than to go over the list and delete people who no longer mattered. That's how I learned that your marriage fizzled—you didn't say so, of course, but the photos of you alone with your cat three years in a row were evidence enough.

Already when the first Cynthia-plus-cat Christmas photo arrived I wondered about your marriage. I brought your card with me so that Ardith and I could gloat together over our Saturday morning coffee. "You have to see this." I thrust your card into her hands. "Quite a comedown from the one with the hunky husband on horseback, don't you think?"

I told her about you and Brown, back in our NPR days, just for the pleasure of sharing my private name for your erstwhile husband. "So I thought of him as Pink," I said. And after a pause: "a pale, right-wing imitation of Brown."

Ardith laughed so long and hard that she got me going too. Everyone in the little coffee shop was looking at us. "Pink," she gasped. "I love you."

We speculated about your motives, about who had ended the marriage, if indeed it was really over, about what made you tick. We imagined Brown telling an exotic wife named Ebony about you and Pink, about how you couldn't maintain a relationship with any color that wasn't pure Republican red. We had a wonderful time.

By the time your third Christmas card-with-cat arrived, the country had re-elected Ronald Reagan because he promised us 'Morning in America'—possibly the most vacuous campaign slogan ever, according to the poets, but as usual we were out of touch. It sounded great, it meant nothing other than an unspecified hope that things would get better. I preferred my update of Keats, which seemed to capture the new American mood: *Democracy is capitalism, capitalism democracy—that is all ye know on earth, and all ye need to know.* The only people who were important in Reagan's America were the rich, the powerful, and the power brokers. People like you. I was irrelevant—my opinions were wrong, I didn't have enough money to matter, and the only power I had came from an electrical outlet. Morning in America.

Around that time my publisher was diagnosed with Kaposi's sarcoma, a rare form of cancer. And then he died, still in his forties, without ever knowing that his death was one of the first in what would become an epidemic of HIV/AIDS, or that the disease would go on to decimate the creative community he had nurtured in the Bay Area. I'm not even sure he ever knew he was dying. I only know that his friends—Ardith, me, all of us—didn't see it coming, despite his looking worse every time we visited.

With his death, I gave up any pretence of writing poetry. I hadn't written any real poetry in a long time anyhow—the odd bit of snarky doggerel, a possibly useful phrase now and then, but nothing that mattered to me in any real sense, nothing worth submitting to a poetry journal, nothing I liked as much as the poems in *The Bureau of Labor Statistics*, nothing the publisher would have considered publishable if he were still alive. I shifted my stack of notebooks from my desk to the back of my closet. And when I went to a bookstore or the library I avoided the poetry section. A cheap thriller, a dark psychological murder mystery, a political rant, anything that confirmed my view of the prosaic venality of humankind—that's what found a home next to my bed.

And as an antidote, cookbooks. I discovered the comfort of reading about food, playing with food—how much easier it was than playing with words that no one cared whether I wrote or not. Alice Waters assured me it was worthwhile—cooking with fresh, virtuously grown local food could be a political act. However insignificant and unacknowledged, I added, silently. I pretended I could improve the world by shopping at farmers' markets. A better world, one perfect organic pizza at a time. It helped that Joy loved the ritual of building a pizza and watching the oven transform it into dinner, especially when her friends were there to enjoy the results. And it had nothing to do with you. I would never invite you for dinner and you would never send gaudy flowers instead of showing up. It felt safer than poetry., although it's only now that I understand that. If I craved escape more than I needed to be part of a bigger world—if I felt duller and more ordinary—at the time I attributed it to circumstances and cynicism and middle aged practicality.

But it kept me occupied, until the Challenger exploded. Of course it was never supposed to happen that way. The launch was intended as a celebration—of American science and engineering and space exploration—of American knowhow and our spirit of adventure— and, in the name of populist culture, of American schoolchildren and teachers, especially those in third grade, because one of the astronauts was a third grade teacher.

For the whole month leading up to the launch, my twenty-nine third graders were caught up in all the hoopla. Their enthusiasm was infectious as they worked on their space projects. We built a miniature solar system with a lightbulb sun and the first four planets rotating around it. We included a moon that travelled in a small circle around the earth, and I taught them about solar and lunar eclipses. We used a tiny blue bead for a spaceship that rotated on a wire around our little blue and green earth, much closer than our moon. We launched baking soda rockets—we even practiced jumping into the air as high as we could, so everyone understood the implacability of gravity and how much rocket fuel we would need to get our spaceship into orbit. The girls and boys wrote letters about their projects and drew colorful pictures on cards that said 'Have a good flight' and signed their names with red and blue crayons and sent them to Christa McAuliffe, the third grade teacher who was now an astronaut. I was proud of every single one of the future scientists and engineers in my classroom.

Which is why, for the morning of the launch, I made special arrangements so all the kids would arrive early to watch the whole thing live on television. The night before, Joy and I lugged our TV to school and set it up on my desk. Once I was back home, I set a second alarm clock to wake me up by six. Joy woke me five minutes before the alarms went off, already excited about her first-ever job as my assistant—I had promised to pay her for helping me, she already knew what she wanted to buy with the money, and she took her responsibilities seriously. It was hard to get out of bed and do all the morning things—I'm not a morning person, never have been—but with Joy's help we arrived at school at eight o'clock, with me hanging onto a hot coffee like it was a life preserver, just as the first kids showed up.

One of the mothers ramped up the excitement by arriving with a rocket-shaped cake made of cupcakes stacked on top of each other., glued together with white icing. It had a Challenger space shuttle, in red, white and blue icing, clinging to its side. The kids wanted to eat it right away. I smiled when Joy said no and then set about guarding the cake as if her life depended on it. I said we would enjoy it later, that we should watch the shuttle get safely into space first. That 'safely' still sticks in my throat—it still tastes bitter.

But at that moment what I felt was satisfaction, seeing the kids' happy anticipation as they gathered on the floor in front of the television, how for the next half hour they sat there with large eyes, captivated, except for the occasional longing look at the cupcake rocket. And proud of Joy as I watched her guide a girl's attention away from the cake and back to the screen. I think I even remember the taste of the coffee, cold by the time I had a chance to drink it, but strong and satisfying. When the rocket lifted off and we could hear people applauding on television, all the children clapped too. I remember enjoying the dramatic end to our space projects as much as the kids.

Less than a minute later the Challenger blew up. It wasn't immediately obvious that we were witnessing a catastrophe. The voice from Mission Control continued reciting what he saw on his instruments as the TV screen filled with white billows that, for a brief moment, resembled Sesame Street's Big Bird. A moment later, as the billow split into two contrails, the trajectory of what might have been the shuttle, tiny against the immensity of the white billows, looked as if it might still be able to go up. But it too lost momentum and curved back in response to the mindless pull of gravity. After long moments of silence, the CNN correspondent picked up the narrative, still speaking authoritatively, talking about the two rocket boosters blowing away, before the Mission Control man said, also with authority, but not quite as much, something about a 'major malfunction.'

In a blur of disbelief, I turned off the television. Some of the children protested, although without energy. I think it overwhelmed all of us, seeing those optimistic and committed astronauts blown to pieces, live and on television.

"Something went very wrong," I said to the children, trying to channel the authority of CNN and Mission Control. "Come up here—I think we all need the biggest group hug ever."

Some of the children rushed to me and hung on like limpets. Joy and the cupcake mother helped to round up laggards, but not before one of the kids knocked down the cupcake rocket and stamped on it, tears of rage brightening his eyes. The mother, thank goodness, gave him a hug all his own, then held him firmly by the shoulders until he merged into the group. Joy prevented others from eating the cake and icing off the floor. And then, for long moments, we were a sloppy, unwieldy amoeba, swaying this way and that. It wasn't even nine o'clock. How were we going to get through this day? I kept hugging—I didn't know what to do next.

Finally someone laughed, the tension fell away, and the children mostly became themselves again.

Over the next day or two, we—like the rest of the country—tried out a variety of coping techniques. Joy brought home jokes. "Do you know what NASA stands for?" she asked. And then delivered the punchline: "Need Another Seven Astronauts." Before I could react, she was on to the next one. "Do you know how they figured out that Christa McAuliffe had dandruff?" Dramatic pause before the new punchline: "They found her Head and Shoulders on the beach."

She laughed at her own jokes. I worried she was coping too well. Then my students told me the same jokes at school, and I forced myself to relax and laugh with them, that it was probably for the best—the jokes provided distance, they made the explosion less real, more like a cartoon.

I decided to ignore the science curriculum and instead taught the children about elegies. I read them a few of my favorites, things like Langston Hughes' *Dream*, which starts: '*Hold fast to dreams | For if dreams die | Life is a broken-winged bird | That cannot fly.*' I introduced them to metaphors, so we could talk about whether space travel was a metaphor, and about what the astronauts' dreams might have been. I asked them to write their own elegies, about the dead astronauts or anything else that made them sad, and they rewarded me with crayoned verses and pictures that reminded me of my first poetic efforts. Best of all was watching them beam each time I pointed out a metaphor one of them had used. By the end of our poetry intensive, after I read them Christina Rossetti's '*When I am dead, my dearest, | Sing no sad songs for me | . . . . And if thou wilt, remember, | And if thou wilt, forget*' and after we talked about when it was okay to stop feeling sad, I felt that we had all earned poetic license to forget.

I think the poetry helped me as much as my students. More, to tell the truth. At home in the evenings I started writing a few tentative poems, the first I'd written in years. I found myself remembering and reliving those other televised deaths and near-deaths from my childhood—the Cuban Missile Crisis, the shooting of President Kennedy and then Kennedy's killer, and that tragic summer when Martin Luther King and Robert Kennedy were both killed. And for some reason that I couldn't fathom, I found myself dreaming over and over about John Lennon, feeling hopeless in front of my television while I saw him shot by crazy men in spacesuits, through endless replays. It struck me that all the deaths I remembered—all the famous deaths—were men's deaths. With the exception of Christa McAuliffe, who died as a token woman.

"Why is it that we care so much more about some deaths than others?" I asked Ardith, after dinner, after Joy was in bed, when we sat down in the living room to finish our wine, leaving the unwashed dishes in the kitchen. "If those same seven people had died in a training accident at sea, it might have had one headline. Or if seven black men were killed in Oakland, nobody beyond Berkeley would hear about it, let alone feel they should mourn."

"I'm not even sure we'd hear about it in Berkeley. But I think you got it right with your kids—we care about a death when it symbolizes an idea—an idea suddenly in jeopardy—in danger of being wrong or false. Those astronauts weren't people anymore—they were metaphors. And I guess if your black men in Oakland turned symbolic, then we'd pay attention to them too—although I imagine fear, or fear disguised as anger, would be more likely than national mourning."

"No—no flags at half-mast for them." I gave her a wry smile, then raised my glass. "Anyhow, to symbols and metaphors—right at the center of things, even when nobody notices."

Ardith laughed. And pulled out a poem she had been working on.

In the aftermath of the Challenger disaster I received a letter from the school board. A Berkeley psychology professor wanted to do a comparative study of third grade students who had seen the Challenger explode and those who hadn't. It would involve a questionnaire for the children, followed by an in-depth interview with the teacher. At the bottom, it listed a name and a phone number for us to call if we wanted to participate. Why not, I thought.

And that's how I met Alex, professor of child psychology and future love of my life. His pheromones wafted across the classroom and swirled up my nose—it was love at first whiff, as I continue to tell anyone who asks. Alex had a lanky, graceful body that practically required hugging—fingers that had a magnetic pull—a sculpted face with deep brown eyes, warm and intelligent behind dark-rimmed, professorial glasses—a thatch of dark hair that flopped endearingly over his forehead. No beard or moustache or sideburns. His voice was deep, almost Middle Eastern, the essence of melodious sex appeal. And even at first glance, I could tell that those lips would taste exquisite. My only worry was that he was too young for me.

Alex's version is different. He still claims he first fell in love with my intelligence. "Imagine having the presence of mind to turn off the television when she did," he would tell people. "And knowing that everyone needed a hug. And then using poetry to help them heal. Of course I had to spend the rest of my life with her." In private, he would say, "I'm just lucky I met you when you were horny enough that you would have fallen for the fish guy if I hadn't found you."

By the time we finished the interview we both knew we had to keep talking. Over coffee he told me he was divorced, no kids. "Three miscarriages—it was more than we could cope with."

I had already told him a bit about my daughter, how indispensable both she and the cupcake mother had been on that awful morning. Now I told him that Joy spent every second weekend in Santa Cruz with her father. We agreed to have dinner together on Saturday. And one thing led to another. *The readiness is all.*

I wasn't too old.

But I wasn't ready to tell anyone about Alex. Not Joy, not Ardith. Definitely not Finn or my family. So when my mother called to tell me that your grandfather had died and that you had decided against a funeral, it was an excellent substitute for everything I didn't want to tell her. She had my full attention.

I understood even then that from your point of view, it was the right decision. Your grandfather was beyond knowing whether he had a funeral or not, or who came or didn't. And it's public knowledge that your interview with Richard Feynman—the noted physicist who unearthed not only the longstanding O-ring problem, but also a history of sloppy science and organizational weaknesses at NASA— was masterful. Alex and I sat on my sofa and watched the two of you unfold a devastatingly clear account of why those seven astronauts died on the shuttle's twenty-fifth flight. It was a fascinating interview—a horrifyingly familiar story that everyone could relate to—every last one of us who has ever worked in an organization where people make bad decisions—and where everyone else, each of us, lets them slide.

With a certain pride I told Alex that I had grown up with you and then worked with you at NPR. I only told him, I realize now, because he said what a good interviewer you were—and because I wanted his praise to include me. Which is why I didn't tell him how, although you were good at your job, even very good, you were also one of those people who trample on most of the people around you.

Which is also why I didn't tell him when my mother phoned me a week or two later with an update to her story. It turned out, she said, that your mother had somehow gotten word of your grandfather's death, despite not having been there for a single visit in all those years since she ran off with her lover. She arrived in a car not very different from the rusted hulk she had driven that long-ago summer, and with an old key she let herself into the house.

My mother was appalled. "You should have seen her," she said. "As round as a dumpling, and her hair was a mess. And she was wearing one of those quilted jackets that made her look even rounder." There was a dollop of distaste in her voice.

We reminisced about how good-looking your mother had been when she was young. And with the smugness of the naturally thin we wondered at how she had let herself go. It's not that hard to push yourself away from the table, one of us would have said, or something like that, and the other agreed in a judgmental moment of mother-daughter bonding. I wish I had thought to ask if your mother had jowls too. Not that it matters who you got them from—it's their existence that matters, at least to me, and I suspect to you too.

The story got juicier. "It looked like she was moving in—a suitcase, big plastic garbage bags full to overflowing, pillows and blankets, you name it. So I decided I had to call Cynthia—your father insisted—we knew her grandfather had left the house to her. And we thought maybe Cynthia would want to see her mother."

But you stayed in New York and instead dispatched a lawyer to straighten everything out, which in your world meant sending your mother packing. It reminded me of those horrid flowers you sent to my book launch. How little effort it took for you to make someone else feel small. Flowers, a lawyer—a minor expense, not worth worrying about, not a real problem. I felt pity for your sad mother.

My mother was appalled that anybody would treat a mother, any mother, like that. "Do you think she was punishing her because she left her behind when she was little," she asked me, "or was it just the money?"

"Maybe both," I said. "Or maybe it was just another thoughtless act—she's turned into such a Republican, she may think of it as asserting her property rights, whether she wants the house or not."

But I quickly forgot about you and your problems. The rest of the eighties vanished while I focused on my own ordinary life—and watched all the bigger events on television. I even missed the big earthquake that devastated the Bay Bridge because I was visiting my mother, who still lived on the outskirts of the middle of nowhere. Not that I really wanted to see a big chunk of concrete crush the cars in front of me, but I nevertheless wondered why I was always someplace boring when the big stuff happened, reduced to watching the drama on television. By the time I got back home, of course, everything had returned to a slightly less convenient version of normal.

But more importantly, the mainstays of my life—Joy, teaching, Ardith, my rekindled interest in poetry—now grew to include my lovely Alex. When I saw my reflection in Alex's eyes, I saw someone who mattered—which fixed so many hurts.

I'm in danger of getting seriously sentimental here, so it's time once again to move on. But before I do, I want to share one of my doggerel poems of the eighties, a poem that still makes me laugh, that I wrote around the time I lost interest in what had for so long been my favorite sport.

The Joy of Baseball

— Going — —

— Going — —

— Gone.

90% of the game is half mental — *Yogi Berra*

NOON FRIDAY: New York City

You fall into the back seat of a cab and try to release the tension from your shoulders before giving the cabbie your address. You realize that after a single hour with your lawyer you're exhausted. And find yourself wondering how hard it will be to sit in court day after day for your trial. If there is one, you hasten to reassure yourself. Not that it helps. The image of all those hours on display, like a mannequin in a store window, your every expression scrutinized for signs of guilt, lingers like a poke in the eye. You have to believe that Jack can—please, please—make it all go away.

To distract yourself you turn to your phone, which greets you with a torrent of alerts from Google and Twitter, plus texts, emails and voicemail notifications. Under the silk of your pretty, innocent scarf you feel the tension tighten its grip on your neck. A lot—far too much—has happened since you turned your phone to vibrate and gave Jack your undivided attention. You know without even thinking about it that good news never, ever, comes in torrents.

You flip through screen after screen of messages, still see references to the Cancer Foundation and Fraud, but attention has shifted to something new: #FakeCancer. When you swear, in your low-pitched, vehement voice, the cabdriver looks at you in the rearview mirror, and a startled, possibly fearful, expression crosses his dark face. In his world innocence is no defence. To be at the scene of an offence—any offence, whether he's responsible for it or not, whether he understands it or not—could change his life. Not today, though. He sees that you're oblivious to him—that you're swearing at your phone. Nevertheless, he speeds up and gets you to your destination as fast as he can.

When you leave his cab, he has to force himself to remind you to pay, because he needs the money even more than he needs to get away from you. You absentmindedly hand him a twenty and tell him to keep the change. You don't notice that there isn't much change to keep.

Your attention is entirely consumed by the clutch of people and cameras in front of your apartment building.

I pledge allegiance / to the flag:
A pay per viewance / to the glog — *Michael Magee*

NOON FRIDAY: Berkeley, CA

A poem starts to shape itself in my head. I'll call it 'pity' and it won't have any capital letters in it—pity will patter on your head. It has a snarky ring to it, and I'm smiling as I come into the kitchen with my grocery bags.

"Joy phoned," Alex says. "She tried to call you. When she heard that Max and his wife were coming for dinner, she said to tell you that she and Liam and Maggie are on their way—and that they'll bring dessert."

"Sorry—didn't hear my phone. But that's great—Max will be happy to see her and we'll have more people to entertain Sarah. How about I ask Ardith to come too—that way we can outnumber the Republicans."

"You do know that we don't have to talk about politics, don't you?"

But I'm already revising my menu—there's enough crab for a nice appetizer, maybe crab and avocado on toasted croutons—some almonds and olives with the watercress and grapefruit for the salad—and if I add some fresh peas and chevre to the asparagus, I'll have a pretty, green pasta primavera—easy—enough for everyone. No return trip to Monterey Market. Giving me plenty of time to write down the first line of my 'pity' poem and see if it leads anywhere before I have to start work on dinner.

Pen in hand, I imagine you feeling sorry for yourself and my poem nearly writes itself.

pity

a soft rain of pity patters on your head
cooling, soothing the hot hurt
until
after dripping
onto your drooping shoulders
and downward, drenching
your arms and fingers
your breasts and belly
your thighs and legs
it puddles at your feet—
sucks you down—
cold

Good start, I think. I'll ignore it for a few days, see whether I'm still happy with it after the pleasure of writing it has faded. I make a note to ask Ardith whether snarkiness has a place in poetry.

And then I check *The New York Times* website, and my day gets even better. There you are again, this time looking straight at the camera. In this photo, your droopy jowls are covered by an artfully knotted scarf. It's your eyes that reveal too much—so black and staring—a paralyzed look, as if you're angry and frightened and, most of all, guilty. I know I'm reading too much into it, but I click on it anyhow, to enlarge it on the screen, to enjoy it fully. That's what I would look like—minus the hidden jowls, of course—if everyone were out to get me. Unbelievable.

It seems that you pretended to have cancer all those years ago—and everyone is wondering why, except for the journalists all over the country who are too busy digging into your other stories, looking for other questionable assertions. Of course you can always dismiss whatever they find as 'embellishments,' or 'misrepresentations'—anything but lies. Anyhow, I'm guessing you don't need me to tell you what now seems obvious, that talking to people who have cancer is different from being the person who's being slashed or poisoned or burned. Did you think that making yourself the victim—cutting out the middleman—becoming the stand-in for all those anonymous cancer patients—made it more dramatic, or more relatable, or was it simple, straightforward attention-seeking? And oh, you put such a brave face on it, back then. A face that people knew and trusted—a face that was worth millions. Not like your face now.

At the end of the article, brazen to the end, you play the pity card. 'Brain tumor' floats out there in a vague sentence that stops short of saying you actually have one, or whether it's malignant. But nice link, Cynthia, to your Cancer Foundation woes. You should know not to talk to the media.

I reread my poem, quite delighted with its timeliness. And then I call Ardith, ask her to come early, to think of some things to talk to Sarah about, and to stop at Acme Bakery for an extra baguette. "Be sure to listen to the news—the Cynthia Lord story just got juicier."

> With liberty and justice for all:
> *With liverwurst / and just / this for all* — *Michael Magee*

The Nineties: Berkeley, CA

Alex had a car. It sounds like a small thing, although these days, with the benefit of another quarter century's knowledge, in the alternative, as the lawyers say, with temperatures rising everywhere, you could see it as a great big planet-eating outrage. But back then, after relying on my feet, my bicycle and public transit for all those years, after not being able to afford a car of my own, it felt like freedom itself. We could go where we wanted when we wanted. We didn't have to consider how heavy something was before we bought it. It felt both luxurious and wrong, all at the same time. We commit our most persistent sins, it seems to me—not just you and me, every one of us, or almost, anyway—when we choose personal short-term benefits over what we know is the right thing to do. I loved Alex and I loved his car—*why not, buy a big goddamn car* (as Robert Creeley said in response to the darkness). So there—I've said it too.

Alex used that car to get me to and from my chemo sessions—sessions that, because my treatment started four days after Saddam Hussein invaded Kuwait, I called my own personal chemical warfare. The car was comfortable. As I got more and more tired, I learned to recline the passenger seat, close my eyes, and just listen to NPR on the way home. The car protected me from all those germs I was supposed to avoid while my immune system was compromised. And I didn't have to confront the stares of strangers looking at me with pity or curiosity when my scarf slipped and revealed my hairless skull.

We were all afraid. Alex, of course, but especially my mother and Max, who had been on the front line during the final, sad year of my father's lung cancer and then the horrible, drawn-out death of Max's first wife. Poor Lisa. And poor Max, who, because he was an oncologist, was the prime target of Lisa's limitless rage. 'What was the point of all that time we spent being poor and never seeing each other, all that time you put yourself and medicine before Julie and me, when you can't even fix your own wife's cancer?' Which, as she weakened, she shortened to 'What's the point?' And then the tears, the attempts at a hug, and the violent pushing away. Deliberately or not, she also pushed away her daughter. Julie ran off to Tibet in search of enlightenment. Or maybe that was Max's fault too, since she's still in Tibet and he never hears from her.

Now that it was my turn, I too worried about my daughter. As my hair fell out Joy invented new ways to spend less time in my presence. More homework, of course, but also shopping expeditions and trips to the library, a return to sleepovers with friends, even rehearsals for a school play that never took place. When she had to be in the same room with me, she twisted her face away out of embarrassment or revulsion. No, it was worse. It was contempt for her so baldly imperfect mother. It was the way you looked at Finn and me in that ethnic restaurant in Washington. What reminded me of that dismal evening was that by then Joy looked like you—that same red hair, maybe a little darker, and a pointy chin that reminded me of yours. And she sounded like you—she fixated on the need to be rich. It was the most important thing she could hope to achieve. As if she were your cuckoo bird, left for me to shelter and feed while you did more important things.

But much as I worried about who or what Joy was becoming, my fatigue and mouth sores and the cramps in my gut were more immediate problems, and they pushed my fears into the background. Or maybe the fatigue and pain were reasons to think that death wasn't the worst outcome—at least it would be over. In the alternative, to invoke the lawyers again, there was the discouraging weight of my conviction that it shouldn't have happened to me. My breasts were small, I was thin, I got regular exercise, I ate vegetables, I wasn't even fifty—I wasn't supposed to have breast cancer. Why me? Why now?

Useless questions, but scary, because they were the gateway to rage.

For distraction I tuned into baseball again, letting myself get caught up in the familiar rituals as the Oakland A's steamed their way to the pennant. It felt like comfort food for my mind, a respite from the life-altering shock of cancer. But when the A's lost the World Series in four straight games, I had tears in my eyes. As though it mattered.

The Gulf War was my other distraction, and it heated up as the World Series vanished into the record books. The war was something I could worry about without it being personal. It was so far away that it didn't seem real. Whenever I couldn't sleep, when no one was playing baseball but I was too tired to do anything else, I could watch the war unfold on television. Of course I understand that using a war for distraction is at least as morally suspect as driving a car. But I couldn't read books—even poetry was somehow too hard, I couldn't concentrate. So instead I watched the war, slumped on the sofa under a cozy afghan, receiving information in disconnected video clips that sounded simultaneously urgent and irrelevant, like a horror flick that I could turn off if it scared me too much.

The war had its good guys and bad guys, always a simple but compelling story arc. Atrocities—looting and plundering, stealing dialysis machines and incubators, beating children with the butts of guns—all inflicted by the bad guys; pain and suffering the lot of the good guys. In October, when a young Kuwaiti girl testified in tears in front of the Congressional Human Rights Caucus about how she had witnessed Iraqi soldiers as they 'took the children out of incubators,' my eyes leaked in sympathy with hers. I teared up again when you interviewed the Amnesty International guy about the two hundred and thirty-two babies whose incubators were stolen by Iraqi soldiers. It was all so sad and hopeless, and I felt so useless under my nice warm afghan.

Alex would hijack the remote and turn off the television. He said I had more important things to do than worry about Kuwaiti babies. He would try to tempt me out for a walk. Or a stroll. Just once around the block. He pointed out that the sun was shining, that it would make me feel better.

"Too tired," I would reply, huddling under the afghan.

"Maybe a meander?"

Me, reaching half-heartedly for the remote: "Why don't you-ander."

Alex, skipping out of reach with the remote in hand: "A we-ander, then—let's go."

We laughed. We went out. And he was right—I felt a little better.

But I always came back to my afghan, where the television and the war were waiting for me. Where the story soon spiralled back to the dead babies. President Bush referred to them time and again, those poor babies who were first 'pulled'—then 'thrown out'—finally 'scattered like firewood across the floor'—each new speech more eloquent, more self-righteous. Your interviews too—not just with the Amnesty International guy but also with Congressmen from both parties and various experts and pundits—used the dead babies as obvious evidence of human rights violations and equally obvious justification for American intervention, which finally happened, quickly and decisively, when American troops drove out the Iraqis and restored the Kuwaiti government. Not to mention guaranteeing Americans access to cheap gas for our cars for the foreseeable future. No, we definitely weren't going to mention that.

My strength was already returning and my head had a fuzz of stubble before we had the first inkling that the dead babies had never existed—not two hundred and thirty-two babies, not twenty-two babies, not a single Kuwaiti baby had been evicted from its incubator. Except in the imagination of a big public relations firm, Hill and Knowlton, hired by the Kuwaiti government the previous summer to get American public opinion on side.

I had grown all my hair back—more grey than brown, and coarser and duller than I remembered, but thick and luxurious nevertheless— by the time the full story came out. Kuwait had paid Hill and Knowlton eleven million dollars. The cheapness of it, considering everything that ordinary Americans lost—over a thousand of our soldiers gave their lives or their limbs or their minds to liberate Kuwait, plus the billions spent by the US government to conduct the war—still strikes me as insulting. The Kuwaiti money paid for a lot of PR and peripheral influence peddling: writing and printing a book for American soldiers, called *The Rape of Kuwait*; subsidizing the

Congressional Human Rights Caucus, which, although it sounded like a legitimate Congressional committee, was nothing more than an ad hoc body where no witness was asked to swear to tell the truth; filming video news reports that looked like real news but were actually press releases in video form; and most importantly, recruiting and coaching Nayirah to tell the Caucus that she had witnessed those babies removed from their incubators. Nayirah, it turned out much later, was the daughter of the Kuwaiti ambassador and never saw what she said she saw.

Fake news. Did you know it was invented and play along, or were you duped the way everyone else claimed they were? In your book you walk an exquisite line between the two options, leaving the impression that the sympathy you felt for Nayirah's story made you gullible at first, but that soon, possibly sooner than anyone else, you began to suspect that everything wasn't as it should be. A soft heart clouded your penetrating intelligence, but not for long. Good optics.

My guess is that you knew all about the fake news, that you maybe even offered advice on how to create those oh-so-skillful VNRs. I wouldn't be surprised if some of the Hill and Knowlton people owed you favors for your part in building credibility. But I'll admit there's not much evidence, one way or the other.

Except that, not long after the revelations of Hill and Knowlton's massive manipulations, NBC decided to replace you with a much younger woman. And then, within days of your departure, you showed up again on your old program to announce that you had bowel cancer, and that you were going public because you wanted to do what you could to encourage early screening.

You looked so brave and beautiful that I felt I should forgive you everything. I sent you a card congratulating you on your bravery. I shared with you that I had gone through cancer treatment and survived, and I was sure you would too. I think I even cracked a joke about your new role as the public face of the all-important poop test, which, now that I think of it, might have been less funny to you than it was to me. I never heard back from you, but of course I didn't expect to—I knew you would feel exhausted.

I worried about you. I wondered whether you would lose all your hair, and whether, once it started to grow back, you would love playing with the stubble on your head as much as I had. I still remember how, at night, waiting to fall asleep, I would rub my head, enjoying the gentle resistance as I rubbed against the grain, and then the silky smoothness when I stroked it flat against my skull. During the day, too, I remember sneaking a feel whenever I could, and how it always soothed me. Hair. How extraordinary. I often wondered whether you felt that strange new connection to your hair. I also worried that you would need a colostomy, and what that would mean for you. I thought about you getting chemo or radiation, and whether there was anyone in your life who would do more than send a card.

But soon your picture and your signature were on every letter the Cancer Foundation sent out, and it appeared that, as usual, you were getting all the help you needed. It was hard to believe, but you were reinventing yourself, even during chemo, as a ground-breaking leader in the crusade against cancer. You clearly didn't need me to worry about you. For months you were featured in newspapers and magazines across the country as the Cancer Foundation's PR people used you to raise awareness and raise money. You were invited to join the Cancer Foundation board of directors, which you graciously accepted in another flurry of publicity. NPR welcomed you back for a visit with a heartwarming interview. The only thing you avoided, after that first appearance on NBC, was television. I assumed—probably everyone did—that you didn't want your public to see you while you were sandbagged by chemo.

"How does she do it? I didn't have the strength to do anything but watch television and worry about dead babies who never existed," I said to Alex after hearing about one or another of your gracious successes.

"People cope in different ways. And some chemotherapies are harder than others. It's not a contest—don't worry about it."

But I did.

Your autobiography was published about a year later, with reviews and interviews everywhere. Your timing was excellent—the nation was ready for a feel-good story about your rise to journalistic stardom, reaching its peak just when you suffered the near tragedy of bowel cancer, which, with your characteristic all-American grit you then turned into the best campaign ever to raise public awareness for the all-important poop test. You wove your uplifting story together with a well-told political account that ran like a red ribbon through the highlights of your own life—every chapter about how you overcame yet more personal or professional difficulties was married to a chapter of serious political analysis. Your book ended up on *The New York Times* bestseller list, where it stayed for a long time.

I should never have bought it—the cover photo, a close-up of a smiling, pre-cancerous, pre-jowls you, should have been enough to dissuade me. Or the title, *My Journey So Far,* with its echo of that old Virginia Slims ad: You've come a long way, baby. Seriously?

I definitely shouldn't have read it, But I was too embarrassed to stand in the bookstore looking for my name, which of course wasn't in the index. The index was reserved for names like Ronald Reagan and Margaret Thatcher, Barbara Jordan and Barbara Walters. So—no doubt like thousands of other forgettable people who thought they knew you—I bought your book and read all the way to the end, thinking, despite the mounting evidence, that I must have been important enough—at least when we were friends back on the outskirts of the middle of nowhere?—for you to add a sentence or two about the hand-me-down clothes, or our Cynthia-and-Michelle pranks and our dreams of the future, or, when you arrived at NPR, how I introduced you to Brown. But even Brown wasn't important enough to show up in your book.

Whatever happened to Brown? Did he too look for himself in your book? No, I can't imagine it—he was too cool and too occupied with his own life to bother. And to his credit, he had anticipated the best way to disappear in the age of Google searches—his name, even capitalized, turns up nothing useful. A university, a college, Facebook and Twitter pages with first names attached, a Wikipedia entry that starts 'Brown is the color of dark wood or rich soil.' Perfect anonymity.

I realize that within that vacuum I can create any future I want for him. So I imagine Brown working in a tropical third world country, a senior NGO administrator with a wry sense of humor that allows him to cope with the untold obstacles and frustrations that so often stymie his good intentions. I see him bobbing and weaving and rolling with the punches, far removed from the parochial concerns of American media and politics. Or maybe, disappointingly, he became conventional. Maybe he owns one of those first names on Facebook or Twitter. Maybe he is easing into retirement after a lifetime as a bureaucrat, or passing on his car dealership to his oldest son so that he can play more golf.

But speaking of parochial concerns, your book irritated me enough to finally goad me into working on a new book of my own. Not the best of motives, of course, but we have to take our motivations where we find them. The title came easily enough: *Major League Baseball and Other American Betrayals*. Not a title destined for the best seller lists, but I liked it. And when I told Ardith about it, she chortled. It was the first and only time I ever really understood what chortle meant. I discovered it was infectious. We joked about how, in a striking blow for gender equality and the inter-cultural marriage of arts and sport, the Baseball Hall of Fame would choose me as the first official poet laureate of baseball.

When Joy heard the title she rolled her eyes, suggested I work on a book like yours instead, a book that people would actually want to read, one that could bring in some money. "But maybe not. The only person you know that anyone else has ever heard of is Cynthia Lord, and her book is already out there. So forget my idea." And off she went yet again, to the library or a rehearsal or whatever. I hoped she would stay away for a long time.

Alex claimed he liked the title—the alliteration, the open-endedness of 'Other.' He liked the combination of specificity and generality. Then he asked to read the poems themselves, but I had to do some bobbing and weaving of my own. "I haven't written them yet—they're still little trails of vapor in my head—the idea for some poems. But they're on the way to being born."

I was wrong. Every poem arrived dead on the page. Often in fragments. A tortured line here, a mangled word there, angry question marks, pointless arrows, black cross-outs. The frustration was palpable, stubborn, wordless. In my head I could see the entire book—a series of poems that cut to the heart of the false promise of the American Myth—but it remained a series of shadowboxes, poem-shaped holes in my brain.

I never told Joy or anyone else, but all I wanted to do was refute the stupid certainties in your book, all that right-wing nonsense about rugged individualism in the faee of adversity that had made me so angry. I knew you would never see my poems. Nevertheless I wanted them to exist in the world—just to be there. But I couldn't write them. None of my usual strategies worked—not the long walks, not my notebook next to the bed to capture nocturnal inspiration, not the forced hour of solitude rereading drafts of old poems, not writing prompts of any sort. I even asked myself what would Yogi do? But the bard of baseball himself remained stubbornly silent.

Ardith refilled my wine glass and then her own. "When was the last time you wrote a poem you really liked?"

Her question stopped me short. "I'm going at it all wrong, aren't I?"

"I guess what I'm wondering is, what does that title mean to you—what are you trying to say?"

"I can't figure out how to make it work—baseball felt like an important metaphor—but I think you're right—I don't care enough." My voice trailed off. I couldn't tell her that my whole project was based on something as flimsy as my irritation with seeing your name forever on the best seller list. But even without knowing the details, she had figured it out. She was right.

I toyed with the idea of blaming my bad poems on the aftereffects of chemo, but I didn't want to lie to Ardith. So when Alex joined us, bringing in a tray of coffee and and slices of kulich, I changed the subject to O.J. Simpson and the trial that was blurring whatever lines we used to draw between news and entertainment and justice and money.

There was so much to talk about—whether the ten women, many of whom were black, and the two male jurors would convict a black man of killing a white woman, whether the women would identify more with the skin color of the defendant or the sex of the victim, whether the police were incompetent or tampered with the evidence (or both), whether a female prosecutor (or anyone on the meagre public payroll) could stand up to the multi-million dollar Dream Team that O.J. had hired to defend him, and whether there really was reasonable doubt that he had murdered his wife. In the end, in the spirit of cosy left-wing wine- and coffee-fuelled camaraderie, we found ourselves wishing that all black men accused of crimes had access to a Dream Team defence, and how if they did, the police might be forced to do their job without the benefit of Rodney King style racism and violence and blatant lies.

As always, you saw personal opportunity in O.J.'s woes. You managed to turn his trial into a key weapon, part of your post-cancer maneuvers to return to the television front lines. Your take on the Not Guilty verdict resonated with a wide swath of middle America. Like them, you assumed he had done it, so—acting like a host instead of a guest pundit on the Sunday morning talk shows—you asked everyone 'What went wrong here?' And they, falling in line with your core assumption, variously blamed the jury for not having the education to understand the forensic evidence, or vilified the choice of prosecutor because sending a woman to stand up to the Dream Team was a losing strategy, or condemned O.J. who, if he weren't guilty, would not have needed his Dream Team to get off. And between the lines and with minimal emphasis, they suggested that maybe the police should have been less sloppy or devious or both. It all made you look good.

The upshot was that the following year, when Fox News was launched as the shiny new thing in right wing media, you became the host of a confrontational Sunday morning program that, with remarkable audacity, they decided to call *Lord Knows*. (No wonder I have trouble with titles, I thought to myself when I heard about it. I'm still not in sync with the times. My own preference would have been to call it *Original Cyn*, but of course you weren't your original self any more.) I ignored your program as best I could, although some of the more outrageous snippets made their way into *The New York Times*, so you continued to infringe on the edges of my life despite my efforts to keep you out.

It didn't help that I saw you live and in person one more time. Alex and I scored last-minute tickets to the grand reopening of the San Francisco Opera because a friend couldn't make it. Ardith helped me put together a festive outfit from a silky sari, all red and gold, that she had brought back from India. She created a design where the embroidered border ran diagonally from my left shoulder, under my right arm and around my back, then across from my hip to my right toe. A few seams and tucks, and like magic the fabric draped around me in an elegant swoop. Alex looked at me and said, "Are you sure you want to go sit in the dark in the opera house when we could go dancing instead?" I pirouetted for him, just to feel the silk flow against my skin.

I was giddy with the prospect of seeing the glamorous restoration of that wonderful old building, of hearing some of my favorite voices, of simply being part of such a festive extravaganza. You must have been an invited guest, probably of some rich donor who bought a table at the pre-performance dinner. Not that you would have described yourself as giddy to be there. More likely for you it was something between opportunity and obligation—what they used to call *noblesse oblige*.

Anyhow. Intermission. A long line for the restroom—beautiful young women in their rainbow finery, middle-aged women who for the most part had succumbed to the glamor of black, and enough women with grey hair for me not to feel out of place. I hummed an aria under my breath, quite content to admire the pageant.

And then I saw you, ahead of me in the line, your blonde hair gleaming above a stunning designer gown, deep red, a shade or two darker than your lips and fingernails. Without thinking, I approached you as though you were a beacon.

"Cynthia, I had no idea you were going to be here." I almost reached out for a hug and an air kiss before I realized you were looking at me with a benign, generic smile—and that you had no idea who I was.

Nevertheless, given the setting, you had to pretend you knew me. "How are you?" you said, eying me and my dress and my grey hair, trying to place me, whether I might be important, or simply as eccentric as I looked. I experienced a moment of seeing myself through your eyes—and was as appalled as you were by my bizarrely incongruous dress.

That's when I should have retreated back to my seat and hung my grey head, waiting for the lights to go down. If I had, I might have enjoyed the rest of the concert. And you would never have remembered me. But I persisted. "I haven't seen you since you and Brown were together. Whatever happened to Brown?"

That's when you remembered who I was. You maybe even remembered my name. I could tell by the way your eyes widened for a moment before your professional mask fell back in place. And hid the disdain or pity or distaste you felt—or whatever it was that caused you to twitch ever so slightly.

"I have no idea," you said. And turned to the woman next to you, a woman wearing a gown almost as expensive as yours, with a question that might have been a continuation of a conversation that I had interrupted.

As you intended, I disappeared back into the concert hall. We had aisle seats, so as the last notes of the final piece faded I could take Alex's hand and slink away, leaving you and the rest of the audience standing and clapping in self-important appreciation for a magical evening.

A little later that same year, Alex and I started our weekly Sunday brunch tradition. We would hang out at Saul's for an hour or two with whichever friends wanted to join us, consuming blintzes and latkes and endless cups of coffee and tea, arguing about politics and psychology and poetry. What I know for certain is that none of us ever considered watching *Lord Knows*. And tha, a few years later, when you and the rest of the country were talking about nothing but Bill Clinton's troubles with Monica Lewinsky, our brunches became a Sunday morning refuge from stupid politicians and the media that obsessed about them. "As if none of them ever made a sexual misstep in their lives," was the way Ardith put it, before biting into a sausage dripping with egg yolk.

Nevertheless, enough other Americans tuned in to make your program yet another of your successes. After considerable gnashing of teeth—and despite my annoyance with myself for caring that you always managed to succeed—I cheered myself up by writing a poem about you. I was even happier when an obscure poetry magazine published it, despite their conviction that it was about a man and a woman and love gone wrong. For me, it was enough to think that maybe, somewhere, there was a reader who understood it.

You, I know, were not that reader, so there's some satisfaction in copying it here:

Between Us

how should we measure
the distance between
us on the edge of different oceans
yet also the space between
your living image and me watching
that image on my big flat TV

how should we measure
the difference between
us—the weight of our words
yours legion, freighted with
fame and fortune—
mine meagre, captive, in an overlooked book

how should we measure
the dissonance between
us—the arc separating
the right on your side and
the stubborn left where
you spent your (misspent) youth with me

what I should measure
is the connection between
us—like DNA helixing too close and
too far—scraping or stretching at
the inflection points too
painful to bear but

too vital to reject

Now, years into a new millennium, rereading my poem, I find
myself wondering why it has always been so important to me that my
poems should matter, why I feel so vulnerable when I write a poem,
and why I worry that it's not important enough, or—worse—trivial,
the way my life feels when I'm vulnerable, which may explain why it's

so hard to write poetry even when I have no choice but to commit words to paper. Do poets care too much? And how do we measure what's too much?

No matter. At least I now understand why I needed to write that poem. It wasn't just that you had once again reinvented a bigger, better career for yourself despite a cancer that sounded more serious than mine, although that obsessed me at the time. And embarrassed me. I couldn't talk to anyone about it. Not to Alex, who I was sure would dismiss it. You're not jealous, are you? he would have asked with sheer surprise in his voice, and I didn't want to tell him that yes I was, because I was afraid it would destroy any illusions he had about me. And I couldn't tell Ardith, who would have insisted on analyzing it down to the root. I didn't want to go there.

I was, I now understand, angry with myself for not fighting to keep on teaching, for not realizing that the kids in my classroom had become a part of who I was. But at the time I thought it was a small thing, just a little job, that it didn't matter. And so I gave in, and let them take away everything I liked about my work.

In my defence, I need to say they ganged up on me.

The first volley, intended only to soften any resistance, came from my oncologist, who gave me his advice in a tiny windowless examining room as I sat naked under the thin blue fabric of a freshly laundered gown. "You shouldn't be around all those children while your immune system is compromised."

"I guess . . ."

The next shot came from my principal. He looked up from the file folder on his desk as I walked in, then blinked to hide his reaction, although not fast enough for me to miss his mixture of aversion and dismay and curiosity. The fuzz of hair that I had admired in the mirror at home suddenly felt freakish, as did my loose clothes, hanging as if they were playing dress-up with my skeleton. Behind his hearty welcome I saw his eyes stray to my chest. I could see him wonder whether my breasts were still there. Or were they pseudo-breasts, surgically rebuilt? Was it one breast or two? Were they stiff and scarred from radiation? I could feel him trying to recall what they had looked like before, and I could sense his lack of memory. He wasn't yet forty and I was nearly fifty. This was the first time my breasts had made an impression on him. I saw him force his eyes back up to my face, I felt how they still contained his silent, awkward inquiry. His eyes shifted again to a spot just below my ear lobe. "We feel it would be easier for you if you moved out of the classroom. It could be part-time for a while, until you feel stronger."

"I'm feeling stronger already . . ."

The administration, in the form of a soft-faced woman with the kind of smile that encompassed all of life's disappointments, delivered the final salvo. "We think that, with all your experience, you could make a real contribution in HR."

"But I . . ."

The way I remember it, none of them asked any questions. They told me what was going to happen. Which is why I didn't feel I had a choice—let alone the energy to resist them—and I didn't think about it. I capitulated.

All of which bothered me even more after you proved—or I thought you did, since I didn't know about your imaginary cancer back then—that I could have had a choice. Once again I chose the easy way out—I blamed you for the way I felt. And wrote a poem.

I wasn't the only person in America to outsource the blame for whatever went awry. Nor was it only me who was oblivious to the things that mattered. As the twentieth century was drawing to a close, everyone else was distracted too, whether by a stain on a blue dress, or the threat of chaos that the Y2K bug would loose on the world, or simply by the extraordinary amount of money to be made by investing in tech stocks. Not a bubble, everyone said. This time is different. Disruptive technologies would change everything for the better—a brilliant Harvard professor had written a whole book about it. A few years later all those clever corporate darlings and the financial folks who had provided the hype would find themselves condemned as the tech boom went bust, but that was still in the future.

Yes, the rest of the world had their own delusions and distractions. Even Alex was caught up in the hype, bragging at dinner that we were ten thousand or forty thousand dollars richer than yesterday or last week or last month, and if I didn't like my job I could simply retire and write poetry, since we didn't need the money anymore.

It's funny how painful memories can hijack a conversation.

"I'm not even fifty yet. And I'm not going to be someone's housewife just because I got cancer."

"Don't you dare play the cancer card with me. Do you even listen? I never said anything about a housewife. Since when is a housewife the same thing as a poet? I thought you hated your job."

"So you don't want to hear about what I do? You don't exactly love the bureaucratic stupidities you put up with either, but I listen to you without telling you to quit your job."

"That's not what I meant . . ."

Long after Alex fell asleep that night, I lay in the dark wondering why I had attacked him. And why he attacked back. I didn't find any answers I could live with.

I spent too much of the rest of the nineties measuring my failures against your successes—how it galled me, the way you soared to ever greater heights while I struggled against the constraints of post-cancerous middle age and the recurring waves of uselessness and tedium that washed over me without warning. In despair I watched my daughter turn into a mini-you, strategizing about college, about her choice of major, about the fastest route to wealth. But I found perverse pleasure in cultivating the fury I felt about the way you and your fellow media stars framed your stories to always, always support the status quo. Although I never did anything useful with all that emotion.

Like when three white supremacists in Texas lynched a middle-aged black man by chaining him to the back of a pickup truck, then dragged him for miles down a country road until he was beheaded by a culvert. Then they picked up the man's severed torso, dropped it off at an African-American cemetery and proceeded on to a barbecue where they celebrated, presumably by getting drunk. Their victim, James Byrd Jr., was a decent man with a saintly family who, with remarkable grace, forgave their father's killers.

The media coverage, yours included, focused on how unbearably grotesque it was, implying that the murder was so far outside the ordinary that there was nothing much to be done—or learned—other than to wring our hands and move on, which is largely what happened. George W. Bush, then the Governor of Texas, couldn't even be bothered to go to James Byrd's funeral.

"Why aren't they connecting the dots? Are they blind to the parallels between James Byrd's killers and Timothy McVeigh? And the Unabomber? And the cops that beat up Rodney King? And all those other stupid white supremacists who think they can do whatever they want?"

"You're right. But I don't think they see any advantage in connecting the dots—more likely they don't see them at all—people don't see what they don't want to see. unless they're forced to."

"What bugs me the most is that whenever a black man commits a crime it's used as a reason to be scared of every black guy in the entire country, but no matter what a white guy does, even if it's as horrific as a lynching, it's inevitably an individual thing—it's treated like some kind of aberration, because we're all supposed to know that white guys are the good guys, just because they're white."

"Maybe I have a vested interest because I'm a white guy, but don't you think maybe you're being too earnest?"

A new thought. What did too earnest look like? How unattractive was it? How was earnest different from concerned or frustrated or completely fed up with the same problems recurring over and over again, as predictable as traffic accidents? And what was the alternative? Lighten up and laugh at life's' horrors, no matter the harm they did? If a lynching wasn't worth being earnest about, what was? Wasn't there something called not earnest enough too?

"I don't think Alex meant any harm," Ardith said over coffee the next day. "I think he's worried about you—that you're taking everything—I don't know—too seriously. No, don't jump on me—" she held up her hand to stop me interrupting. "That's not what I meant. It's more like all your worrying isn't helping you—you have to look after yourself too. He's concerned about you. We all are."

"So I've turned into a humorless old crone. Have you talked to him about this?" I would have loved to keep the accusation out of my voice, but I couldn't do it.

"Of course not. So prove to me that you're not a humorless old crone—although I think maybe you already have, just by coming up with that line." We laughed, sort of, and moved on.

In the larger world too, buoyed perhaps by the soaring stock market, people laughed and moved on, ignoring possible warnings despite alarms that clanged for attention. For instance, the murky connections between the CIA's training of foreign soldiers to fight the Soviet forces in Afghanistan, the bombing of the World Trade Center parking garage and the rise of Al Qaeda. Or the growing divergence between rich and poor, white and black, Republicans and Democrats, and, except for a few scientists, anything at all about global warming. A new century was coming, a new millennium—why not be optimistic?

Half the lies they tell about me aren't true. — *Yogi Berra*

FRIDAY, EARLY EVENING: New York City

Your building has a good address, although the view from your apartment is nothing special. You can't see Central Park because your small one-bedroom unit is on a lower floor and faces the wrong way. Nevertheless you stand at the window looking at nothing for a long time. You've spent the afternoon going through emails, far more emails than you had any memory of sending or receiving, emails that tell too much or too little of the story, emails open to misrepresentation.

Chaotic thoughts, questions, ideas, and feelings surge through your mind—but each one is no more than a fragment, the sort of half-baked nonsense my friends and I, back at Penn in the sixties, called a cept, because it was half a concept, but still good enough for a B in most of our courses, unless the professor expected more of us. Though you haven't worried about B's or grades of any sort for a long time, and cepts won't serve you well in the current situation.

Yet there they are, a shifting kaleidoscope, taking shape as swirling shards of people: an unctuous pharmaceuticals man, your ex-husband, an NBC executive in a moment of rage, Barbara Walters, Brown, Hill and Knowlton people, Cancer Foundation people, journalists and reporters and anchors, physicians, studio audiences, Fox News people, politicians, your lawyer. And sharp edges of random words: no and why and who and what now, and everyone, and normal, and who did it hurt, and then back to why. You always come back to why.

And why now. You feel your own rage, and it lasts far longer than a moment.

You consider destroying your computer. It would be so easy. Go up to the roof and toss it. Or throw it into the river. Or drown it in the bathtub. But you know that would make you look guilty beyond a shadow of a doubt. And besides, those emails will persist. In other people's computers. In random locations everywhere in the menacing cloud. So not an option. You grit your teeth.

I would love to leave you there, feeling sorry for yourself, seething with your incoherent rage at all the people who treated you badly. But that's not what happens.

What happens instead is that you turn away from the window. Get a grip, you say to yourself. You repeat it out loud: get a grip. And then you realize you're hungry and that your descent into despair is nothing but low blood sugar. You haven't eaten since breakfast, and breakfast was nothing but a container of yogurt. You find a frozen steak in the freezer, and for the first time in days you laugh—a laugh at the absurdity of the world. Red meat, you think. Perfect. And pop it in the microwave to defrost. You're tempted to pour yourself a drink, but you know that's the wrong thing right now.

The ordinariness of chopping shallots and watching them sizzle in the frying pan, of making a salad, of searing the steak, every step of making your dinner intensifies your hunger, and also reconnects you with your resolve. You gobble your food as though someone might come and take it away from you, and then, fortified, you ask yourself what the worst case scenario would be. A guilty verdict, you tell yourself. Prison. It happened to Martha Stewart, it could happen to you. And if Martha could get through it, then you can too. Just for fun, or to ward off a new wave of despair, you imagine arriving at prison with orange hair and fingernails, and you fantasize about writing a prison memoir that will pay for a bigger apartment on a higher floor, with a view of Central Park. It would work, if it came to that.

But you won't, can't, let it come to that. You need to figure out how to take control of the situation and change the outcome. The key, you realize, is that, at least for the moment, it's not a legal problem. It's a communications problem—only if you get it wrong does it become a legal problem. And you're as good as it gets when it comes to communications problems.

You clear the table, grab a legal pad and four pencils with sharp points. You draw circles on the pad — each circle a problem— Cancer Foundation Fraud—allegations, you add, with a hint of a smile—Fake Cancer in another circle—First Class Airfare in another—you press the pencil in the next circle, force yourself to write Wine Auctions, not wanting to admit it too could be a problem. And besides, that was so long ago. The point breaks. With a new pencil, you finish the word.

Then you scribble out the remaining circles. If there are any other issues, they're subsets of the four you've already identified. Under each circle you jot the questions you would ask if you were interviewing someone in your situation—someone you wanted to expose as a self-serving fraudster on national television—someone you needed to ask tough questions.

QUESTION: Usually when someone is facing possible criminal charges they don't talk to the media. Why are you here?

ANSWER: You know, [NOTE—must talk to a man—not Fox, that would look too incestuous—NBC? CNN?] at least for the moment, the only court that I'm being judged in is the court of public opinion. I've talked to a lawyer and he tells me there's unlikely to be an indictment. And you're right—you know how lawyers are—they tell you to say nothing except 'no comment' and 'I want my lawyer.' But when the only place you face charges is in the court of public opinion, then it seems to me that, unless you're guilty [NO, never use that word] unless you have something to hide [NO, not hide, another word to avoid] you owe it to everyone to tell the truth.

QUESTION: So what is the truth about the fraud allegations? You've been accused of helping drug companies unload expired cancer drugs so they could claim tax breaks.

ANSWER: That's a great question—it's the question I'd ask if I were in your chair, although I'm not sure I'd have the guts to lead with it. Anyhow, one answer I could give you is simply to point out how improbable that would be. Because I know nothing about cancer drugs and even less about corporate tax strategies. But let me walk you through what really happened.

Some years ago I sat next to a pharmaceutical executive on a flight to Los Angeles, I think it was. He recognized me, we got talking, and although I don't remember for sure, I imagine I mentioned my connection to the Cancer Foundation, because it was—and is—important to me. He asked me how he and his company could help. Quite frankly, I was surprised that his company wasn't already a major donor—but back then the Cancer Foundation was more focused on individual donations. One thing led to another, and the next time he was in New York I set up a meeting. It went well, and the board encouraged me to contact other drug makers. Somewhere along the line, someone introduced the idea of Gifts in Kind—basically, donations of things rather than money—but as a board member I wasn't involved in any of the details.

QUESTION: But even if what you say is true, aren't you concerned that you set in motion a plan to give expired cancer drugs to patients?

ANSWER: That does sound terrible, doesn't it? It would be like giving your child a glass of milk from a carton you bought a month ago. But you know what? Pills and milk aren't the same. A few nights ago, I had a headache. I don't get headaches very often, so when I looked for some Tylenol in my medicine cabinet, I found that it had expired in 2008—seven whole years ago. But it was late, my head hurt, I didn't want to go out to get new pills, and there wasn't any funny-looking green fuzz on the pills, so I took one. And you know what? My headache went away and I got a good night's sleep. And it made me think about the whole notion of drug expiry dates. Again, I'm no expert, but it seems to me the drug companies are required to demonstrate that their pills are stable for a certain amount of time. So they put them on a shelf, or whatever, and then every once in a while they test them to make sure they're still okay. But they don't want to wait seven or ten years to see if their pills are still stable. After a year or two, they say, that's long enough—we know they're safe for a year or two—and so that becomes the expiry date. Besides, they don't really want people like me to hoard their pills forever. They want us to look at the expiry date, throw them away, and buy new ones so that they can sell more pills. So that's kind of a round-about answer to your question. But no, I don't think that these drugs are like a carton of milk that goes off after a few weeks in your refrigerator.

QUESTION: Did you ever accept money from a pharmaceutical firm?

ANSWER: Yes, of course I did—because they were charitable donations. I sold them tables at charitable dinners, I accepted their money for silent auction items—when someone gave me a check for the Cancer Foundation, I accepted it. [Stop here if possible—NO— need to defuse the bomb before they launch it]

I was also asked to provide some executives with media training— I guess they thought I knew a thing or two about interviewing—and they paid me for my work.

QUESTION: But couldn't that be seen as a conflict of interest?

ANSWER: I don't follow—how does getting paid to do a job become a conflict of interest? There are millions of people in this country who have paid jobs and also volunteer with charities— whether it's their child's baseball team or the Cancer Foundation or whatever—and I don't think they're in a conflict of interest. Although maybe calling strikes when your son or daughter is pitching could qualify . . . . [Nice misdirection. Don't overdo it.]

QUESTION: About those silent auctions at those charitable dinners: people are saying that the Cancer Foundation's rare wine auctions are nothing more than a scam to give rich donors very large tax receipts by over-valuing the wines. Could you explain?

ANSWER: That question should probably be directed at a wine expert or an economist instead of me, but let me try. Some wines are better than others, and they cost more, just like some cars cost more than others. But speaking of good wine, I want to share a story about a writer, musician and very brave man named Paul Quarrington. On learning that he had terminal lung cancer, his response to the fates that were ending his life too early was something like 'okay, no more cheap wine—let's enjoy the next few months'—and his creativity soared even as it was burning out. And I hope someone gave him a bottle of very good wine.

But getting back to rare wines, after a number of years, when most of a particular good wine has been consumed, whatever few bottles are left in the world earn the rare wine label. And by then some people are willing to pay more to get their hands on one. This is good for charities, because if you can get a lot of people who like rare wines into the same room, you can encourage them to raise their bids because the money is going to your charity. The more they pay, the better for the charity. And if you're lucky, you can convince the buyer that, after they've owned the bragging rights to a special wine for a year, instead of drinking it they should donate it back to the charity and let us auction it off all over again—and that way the charity gets more money for research and treatment of cancer patients. So if you happen to have a bottle of rare wine, and you want to support that charity, if you donate it you should get a tax receipt, just as if you had given them a check. It's like donating an old car to NPR, except that it's easier to deliver.

QUESTION: Rumors are flying all over the internet that you contrived your own cancer diagnosis. What's up with that?

ANSWER: Here's the full story, and you're the first to hear it. Let me start by saying that I like to think of myself as a rational, objective, analytic person, so this is all a bit embarrassing, but here goes. My doctor used the word cancer. I was scared, as most of us would be when we hear that word. And in that moment I wasn't rational, or objective, or analytic. I was quite simply scared to death. Whatever his exact words were, what I heard was that I had cancer of the colon. A few days later I went on television to talk about the importance of early screening. And the next thing that happened, the Cancer Foundation asked me to be a spokesperson for early screening, which I was happy to do because I realized—literally in my gut—how important early screening is if we want to save people from dying from this dreadful disease. I can't remember exactly when I finally learned that what I had was possibly or even probably only pre-cancerous polyps, but by then I already thought of myself as a cancer survivor, and even if it isn't literally accurate, it's emotionally true. I was scarred by cancer, as far too many people are, and I want to use that experience to sympathize with every single person who has ever had to face a cancer diagnosis. And to help raise money for research and treatment, because it's so important.

You read your answers out loud to hear how they sound, marking your script with a red marker where it needs emphasis or improvement. You're pleased that most of it, to your ear, sounds sincere and friendly and honest. You're least happy with the money question—you know in your now-famous gut that the real questions will be tougher, will use the word fraud, or bribe, more often. You put a big red X through that part of the script. It needs a rewrite, although some of it is useable. Overall, I imagine you would give yourself a B, if your were thinking in terms of a grade, which you're not.

What you're thinking about is that it's late. For now it's best to sleep on it. Before going to bed you pour yourself that drink and sip it slowly while looking out the window. You've earned it, you tell yourself.

> I pledge allegiance / to the flag:
> *I plug elegance / two thief rag* — *Michael Magee*

FRIDAY, LATE AFTERNOON: Berkeley, CA

"Fake cancer? You've got to be kidding me." Ardith walks into the kitchen brandishing a baguette in one hand and a bottle of white wine in the other. I have a fleeting image of an exuberant Brunhilde. "What was she thinking? Why would anyone want to pretend they had cancer?"

"We don't know for sure that she did. Thanks for picking up the baguette—and the wine too—this will be perfect with dinner. Can you shell the peas?" I store the wine in the refrigerator, then hand her a bowl and big bag of peas in their pods.

She perches on a stool at the counter. "But let's say that she did— what reasons can you think of? Give me three—right off the top of your head." The first peas ping into the bowl.

"Let's see—wasn't she kicked off her show just days before she told the world she had cancer—so maybe the cancer was a cover-up for being fired? Or" —I'm thinking as I chop the woody ends off the asparagus—"she went off to have cosmetic surgery and had to hide from public view, but felt she needed something more serious to explain why no one saw her. Or"—I turn toward her and mime pulling a rabbit out of a hat—"I've got it—number three—this has to be it. She had a cancer scare—a polyp or some such—and decided that she could get more mileage out of it by pretending it was the real thing."

"I like it. But I like your cover-up idea even more. After all, wasn't that all around the time when Bush the First sent the troops into the first Gulf War? And there was that scandal about news manipulation? Cynthia could definitely have been part of that, don't you think?"

"And if the network found out about it, they would have had to get rid of her. And then figure out how to bury the evidence."

"The Cancer Cover-up—doesn't that sound like it should be a murder mystery?"

"You know, when I first heard she had cancer I actually felt sorry for her—thinking about her coping with chemo and a colostomy and all that all on her own. And then she managed to do so much—so much good stuff—while supposedly getting treatment. As opposed to me, sitting around like a lump for all those months. I still remember how hard it was to get up and brush my teeth. And how stupid and inadequate I felt when Cynthia was out there doing all that fundraising. I just couldn't imagine where she found the energy." I shrug and make a face to make myself sound less maudlin.

"So maybe it's not a murder mystery—maybe it's a heartbreaking masterpiece about the lies and betrayals of the rich and famous."

"I think I've got enough avocado and crab for about two dozen croutons. Would you rather make the croutons or do the avocado?"

"You look like you need to smash something—you get the avocados." I pass Ardith the bread knife and cutting board, then start scooping the avocados. We work in silence, concentrating on the food. And giving me time to think. As usual, Ardith is right. And subtle. I love the way she channels Emily Dickinson. *Tell all the truth, but tell it slant* —

But we should also serve the truth straight up, at least to ourselves, even—or especially—when it's less than palatable. I need to ask myself why, of all the people in the world, the only person whose imminent downfall makes me want to gloat and glory and dance with delight is Cynthia Lord's. What does that say about me, that I crave her disgrace? I can feel myself resisting, looking for excuses to think about something else, or at least to postpone my moment of reckoning with myself. But I also need to understand why she has always made me feel small, how she manages to do it without so much as giving me a thought.

Maybe it isn't her. It's me. I do it to myself. I've been doing it all along. How obvious. But I've never realized that before. Do we all do it to ourselves, I wonder, or am I some kind of weird anomaly?

And all these years I've pretended to be some kind of a poet, while remaining utterly oblivious to the fact that Cynthia is nothing but a symbol, a metaphor, for something I don't want to confront. But this is definitely not the right time—it's too late, too soon, too something—I won't think about this now. I have guests arriving any minute. And for the moment, for this irrevocable moment, I want to enjoy smashing my avocado into a pale green paste named Cynthia Lord. And anticipate adding the lemon juice, mixing it in, and imagining how it stings. Make of it what you will. A symbolic symbol. A meta-metaphor. Yes.

With liberty and justice for all:
with lip hurting / and just this / for all — *Michael Magee*

The Twenty-First Century: First Decade

The only good thing about my mother's death was that she died before the Twin Towers came down. By the end she was so anxious, so easily upset by the smallest disruption, that we were all, I think, grateful that she was spared that final catastrophe.

The election was bad enough. She had been living in Florida for years by then, and the butterfly ballots and hanging chads and voter disqualifications and all the other electoral chicanery that led to George W. Bush becoming President felt deeply personal to her. It didn't help that she had friends who knew Katherine Harris, who was Florida's Secretary of State and, more importantly, the woman who handed the election to Bush.

"I never really liked her," my mother told me. "There was something phoney about her, and I avoided her when I could. But I assumed she had some sort of a moral compass—most people do. I never thought she was capable of election fraud." If only I had known about your fraud back then, I find myself thinking. The parallels might have given her a sense of perspective, or lessened her sense of betrayal. But we didn't know, and she remained fretful.

By then the cancer had spread to her liver and spine, and the pain made her anxious because she could never predict when it would get worse or where it would hurt next. So of course she wasn't in the mood to laugh and shrug off political stupidities, especially outrageous ones. But she was also stating the obvious, at a time when even the Supreme Court tied itself in knots to avoid that particular truth.

"He's going to be the worst President ever," she said more than once as she lay suffering, with a prescience I wish she had been spared. The response she liked best was, 'I hope you're right,' which always earned me a smile. A smart woman. A good woman. I loved her so much.

She looked exhausted, her pale face etched with the strain of dying. I offered morphine, but she insisted that a couple of Tylenols was all she wanted. She swallowed them with difficulty. I held her hand and she rewarded me with a look of gratitude before she closed her eyes and, I hoped, slept. I stayed with her, to watch her looking peaceful, but mostly to hold onto her hand as long as I could, while it was still warm.

Maybe she was fretting about the election because it distracted her, because it was something that people should be able to make right, unlike her failing body. Or maybe she believed that if the election could be repaired then she could be fixed too. But I couldn't force myself to ask her the simple question that was stuck in my head: why do you still care? I suspect I was afraid of her answer. And now again I see the parallel. I see it's the question that Alex has been asking me—but this time I'm the one keeping the answer to myself.

By the time Max and I finished the work of emptying and selling her condo, I had had more than enough of death and taxes and especially Florida. Max, on the other hand, with nothing but work and an empty house to go back to, insisted that we spend one last weekend there—to enjoy the beach, he said. To avoid having to deal with the reality of his empty house, where none of his lost family would ever visit him again, I understood.

So I called Alex to tell him I had to stay a few more days—that Max couldn't face going back to his life yet. Alex asked whether I had any room left in my life for him—was I ever coming back? And we had the kind of fight that couples have when one partner has to neglect the other, not out of anger, but because of a prior claim—and the neglected one is expected to cope with a grace that's impossible to muster.

I endured the fight with Alex because it seemed to me that Max needed me more, needed me to stay, to listen to him talk about his losses—our dead mother, of course, but more importantly, the earlier, less normal losses of wife and daughter—the way Lisa's cancer kept growing and spreading like her anger at dying too soon, and how Julie, still lost in Tibet or somewhere else, didn't even know for sure that her mother was dead, let alone her grandmother, and probably never would. But it turned out that Max had really meant it when he said that what he wanted was a few days on the beach. That, and evenings spent drinking banana daiquiris and telling bad jokes.

On my flight home I wrote apologetic poems to Alex.

"I should have left as soon as we finished the paperwork," I told him as soon as I saw him. "I won't ever, ever, do that to you again."

"You mean when your next mother dies?" Sarcasm? Humor? A bit of both?

I played to the humor. "I'll ignore it completely—she can die on her own—or Max can look after everything." Later I reread my poems, recognized how pitiful they were, and fed them through the paper shredder to be irretrievably rid of them.

I had taken an extended leave of absence to be with my mother, and after she died I couldn't come up with a single reason to return to work. Certainly not the money, now that Joy had graduated—with a degree in physics and engineering—and was offered a signing bonus to entice her to accept a high-paying tech job. She would get rich all on her own.

Life was too short to waste another eight years, I told myself, and then Alex. Eight long years trying to extricate myself from human resources. From forms and regulations and tedious training sessions and interventions to encourage principals and teachers to appreciate each others' points of view. And always, always obstacles in my way: 'enrolments are shrinking, there's no room this year'—'the union is pushing back, we're powerless'—'it's always hard to return to the classroom'—'we need you for this special project that you're perfect for'—'I think we'll be able to swing it next year.'

Talking with Alex, I finally realized why I couldn't face going back to work. And what the real problem was—there was no next year., there never would be a next year. I was useful to them in HR and they didn't want the hassle of replacing me. Or they wanted younger people in the classroom—people they could pay less. By then the oldest third-grade teacher in the system was seven years younger than me, and all the rest were clustered in their twenties and early thirties. None of them with a history of cancer.

Just after school would have started if I were still working—well, of course, school did start, simply without me—those planes demolished the World Trade Center and everything got worse. Anger, fear, nationalism and xenophobia rampaged across the country, aided and abetted by the media. You included. As usual, you already knew what American viewers wanted to see and hear, and you polished and packaged your commentaries and interviews to make them look attractive and new. The viewers, of course, were hungry for what you gave them, and they liked you even more.

You made everyone's anger and impotence and outrage look natural and right. How could an upstart group of extremists with nothing but hatred and a willingness to die for their dogma manage to breach the enormous Atlantic moat that had kept our country safe from attack throughout history? How dare they? You personified their righteous indignation, served it up with subtle undertones of racism; you did it with a veneer of all-American authority that deflected questions and counter-arguments. I wish I could go back and analyze—or even just describe—how you did it. But all that's left in my mind are vague impressions, now no doubt diluted and mutated by time.

What I remember far more clearly is that I was incapable of feeling what you and all those other Americans seemed to feel. And how upsetting it was to be so profoundly out of step with everyone. I lacked the depth of rage that I saw on display on television—and I couldn't share the jingoism that made the outrage so ugly. What I felt was closer to sadness, or maybe emptiness. I couldn't stop thinking about the bereaved, all those women and men and children who had lost people who mattered to them. I discovered that I envied the dead, like my mother, who didn't need to see what was happening to the country, to the world at large—how revenge and righteousness had swamped every more generous impulse.

What I did was to pull back. At first, after my mother died, after I turned my back on Human Resources, I thought I would look for a job with substance, or maybe go to graduate school, that I would find some new and better way to connect with the larger world. But instead, without ever making a conscious decision, I found myself focusing on what was small, immediate, positive, and most of all, personal. Alex, friends. Cooking. And to my surprise, gardening.

Our long-neglected garden became an antidote to my despair. It helped remind me of my mother, whose only regret on moving to Florida had been that she lost her beloved garden. Hers had been pretty and pleasant, although I had never fathomed the depth of her pleasure. Now it felt important to carry on what she had done. Instead of dinner conversations about work or politics or war or even poems, I shared what I had learned about plants and garden design. I envisaged a lush oasis in our back yard, with deep shade and tiny, shade-loving flowers and a perfect Zen-like waterfall. I imagined two bright red Adirondack chairs with wide arms waiting for a cup of tea or a glass of wine, an inviting place to talk or read books. Plus a small, sunny spot for herbs and tomatoes. Flora, I announced, were much less problematic than fauna—especially human fauna.

Over the next few years, I managed to turn the garden into something nicer than it had been, although I never achieved my perfect vision for it. Then, as my sadness around my mother's death and the deaths of all the victims of 9/11—as well as the deaths of unlucky soldiers we sent to avenge the earlier deaths and all the poor Afghanis and Iraqis we bombed in retribution or as collateral damage—when all those dead were silted over with time and distance, the reality of gardening as hard work and dirty hands and a sore back trumped my early ideal. It wasn't enough for me anymore, the unending struggle to turn a small patch of recalcitrant earth into something prettier. There were more compelling things to do and talk about. Fauna once again won out over flora for space in my head. And now, after four years of drought, my garden is once again scruffy and neglected. As if in compensation, I occasionally receive congratulatory letters from the water people because I'm so good about using less water.

What eventually expelled me from my garden retreat was Hurricane Katrina. Watching the horror of New Orleans unfold made me far too angry to find any residual satisfaction in the slow pace of plant life. No, that's too glib—it's not nearly true enough. Here's what's true: watching you made me angrier and angrier. You had the audacity to make the catastrophe all about you. You reported on nationwide television how painful it was to see a body float by your luxury hotel in the French Quarter. You described sleeping on the floor of your room in your luxury hotel, huddled between the window and the bed, so that your room would look unoccupied as the hotel was overrun by terrifying gangs of armed young men—men who you couldn't actually see because it was so dark with the electricity off, it was as dark as their skin. And you implied, without, of course, specifying, that these dark marauders in the dark were, inevitably, intent on rape and pillage.

And yet, somehow, despite the terrible conditions you were working under, somehow your minions always found electricity for the lights and cameras and transmission lines to feed your words and image to your hungry public. You always looked your best—clean designer clothes, clean blonde hair as carefully styled as if you were in the studio, full make-up and even those perfect red fingernails so that you looked the way we expected you to look—as if you had made an extraordinary effort just for us. I'd thank you, except for the racism.

The racism, as I said, made me angrier and angrier. The way you reported on deserving, resourceful white survivors 'finding' supplies, while undeserving black 'looters' took stuff they weren't entitled to and made everyone feel unsafe. Even the National Guard would only enter the flood zones in full battle gear, rifles at the ready, as if they were scared of some drowned black zombie reaching up out of the floodwaters and grabbing them by the balls and pulling them under. Which was the main story. Unlike the other story, the one about those twenty thousand underclass Americans who, even though they were overwhelmingly black, felt they deserved better than to be treated like prisoners in the Superdome, suffering in the unbearable heat and the stinking dark without enough water or food, without any information about what was going on. Instead, you—and, in fairness, all the other journalists too—fed us rumors and accusations and justifications about unspeakable violence and rapes, even of babies, which were repeated as headline news, although none of it was ever substantiated. Not that it mattered—by the time the truth became public it was a footnote, not a headline.

Another footnote was that your luxury hotel was on high ground, so that no body could have floated by for you to see. It also turned out that there was no corroboration for your stories about violent gangs that frightened you while the lights were out. Now though, thanks to all the stories about your alleged frauds, these stories are finally getting the attention they deserve. The current narrative is that you likely never let the truth get in the way of telling a good story—and that there was never a story so big that you couldn't reframe it so that it was all about you.

Back then I didn't know you were lying. What bothered me most was the unstoppable, unthinking, knee-jerk racism—that blatant, gut-level fear of poor black Americans—that tainted every perspective of the Katrina story. As if they were the enemy.

"It's all so awful—Bush pretending it isn't happening, FEMA too busy covering their pure white bureaucratic butts to do anything useful—and all those people dying. It breaks my heart." I was driving Ardith to her appointment with her doctor, where she was going to learn whether she had cancer. I should have been telling jokes, I suppose, trying to lighten her mood. But jokes felt wrong. Besides which, I couldn't think of anything remotely funny. Hurricane Katrina was grim, but it was also a distraction from whatever was happening in Ardith's body.

She shifted to turn toward me, an almost smile on her lips. "You remind me of when you were getting chemo and all you could worry about was those dead babies in Kuwait. Are you going to obsess about this too?"

As long as you don't have cancer, I wanted to tell her. I didn't mean to remind you of cancer, I wanted to say. "You know, I think I am," I said instead, keeping my eyes on the road ahead of me and my tone light.

Because Ardith wanted me to go in with her, we both heard the news together. No cancer, the doctor said, just dysplasia—abnormal cells, but not cancerous. "We'll keep monitoring you, obviously, to be on the safe side, but I'm cautiously optimistic. What you need to do now is stop worrying." The doctor looked at me. "Make sure she gets lots of vegetables and fresh air and exercise, and she should be fine."

I remember how I blinked away tears before promising fervently to follow through on her prescription. And how Ardith's face smoothed as the tension of the last few weeks drained away. She thanked the doctor as though she had personally cured her with extraordinary skill and dedication. Her eyes looked damp too.

As soon as we got outside, we hugged each other long and hard. "You know what? Let's stop at the farmers' market on the way back and get lots of vegetables. And then we'll go cook something special and open a bottle of wine to celebrate. Alex is going to be as glad as we are."

The two of us made the greenest lasagne ever—we added raw spinach and chard to the pasta dough, so that when we cooked it it turned bright emerald. We used the rest of the greens, and broccoli rabe as well, for the filling. And garlic and lemon zest and herbs and cheeses. We took our time, stopping for cups of green tea so we could bask in the happiness of a healthy verdict. I pushed Katrina to the back of my mind. I wouldn't let it darken this private celebration.

The lasagne was in the oven and we were just finishing our tea out on the deck when Alex arrived with a chilled bottle of Champagne. With a flourish he sent the cork flying to the far end of the garden, then caught the foaming wine in three glasses.

Santé was the first word of his toast, a toast that went on almost as long as a wedding speech, full of funny jokes and heartfelt emotion. It might have gone on even longer, but Ardith finally held up her hands. "Enough already. I'm not dead yet—although if you keep going I might die of embarrassment."

"Michelle, did you record my speech? I might need to recycle it for the eulogy. And you should get to work on a poem—Poet Avoids Cancer Only to Die of Embarrassment."

"That could be the headline for the obituary—especially if the *National Enquirer* runs it—but I don't think it works as a poem."

"Get serious—*The Enquirer* doesn't even know that poets exist—and they're not going to start running obituaries for poets—their readers would complain. Besides, it would make a great poem—don't you think, Ardith?"

"I'll be dead by then, won't I? So the two of you will have to fight it out. Or get a divorce. Now there's a headline: California Couple

Divorce over Poetry Dispute. Or is that a poem?"

We continued playing all through dinner. The Champagne bubbles—and our profound relief about Ardith—made us giddy, silly, happy.

But that night, around two or three in the morning, I woke up thinking again about Katrina. And got up to write a furious poem that I called One Thousand Eight Hundred and Thirty-Six Deaths. Tomorrow I should look for it. It could be the core of a new, better poem about that floating dead body you felt you had to conjure up. Although first I need to figure out why one thousand eight hundred and thirty-six deaths weren't enough for you.

What you should know is that, even as I was pouring my feelings into that poem, my embarrassment grew. When my poem failed, despite my good intentions, I was forced to confront my own ignorance—and the queasiness I suddenly felt about living in America for nearly sixty years without ever knowing much about black lives, except for the headlines. Or about black poetry, except for maybe Langston Hughes and Maya Angelou. And I didn't know much about them either.

I hadn't gone to Washington, D.C. when Martin Luther King shared his dream. I hadn't marched in Selma. I watched it all on television, and when the Civil Rights Act was passed, I moved on. Even as a teenager I must have known that racism hadn't been fixed, but I think I assumed that things—elusive, unspecified things that I didn't bother to think about—were moving in the right direction. And whenever there was evidence to the contrary over the years, evidence I couldn't ignore, like the Rodney King beating and the acquittal of all four police officers who were caught on film doing the beating—when things like that happened, I lashed out at the individual racist perpetrators. In my mind they were to blame—individual wrong-headed cops and jurors—but I thought of them as an ignorant minority, people too old to know better, people who would die soon and leave the country a better place.

Admittedly, part of the problem was that I'd grown up in an all-white suburb on the outskirts of the middle of nowhere, but there were some black students when I went to Penn, and then I had known Brown in Washington, although never as well as you did—and while I don't remember meeting any black people at all in Santa Cruz, I had had black students in my classes in Berkeley—and I had often talked with their mothers and sometimes their fathers too. There had been black colleagues at school over the years. But not a single one of those relationships had ever grown into friendship, and definitely not into mutual understanding. I had never made the effort. I had always, just, simply, moved on.

The morning after my failed poem, I didn't even need my second coffee to realize that my embarrassing ignorance wasn't going to go away by itself. I told Alex about what had happened in the middle of the night, how my poem had crashed and burned because I didn't know what I was writing about, how stupid it made me feel.

He took his time pouring us both another coffee before saying anything. "You know, there's a new guy we just hired—an African-American from Boston University—who's done some really interesting work in psycholinguistics—he's part of the Center for Race and Gender too—I think you'd like him. Why don't I invite him and his wife for dinner? Or—you could audit an Afro-American poetry course—I think you would learn a lot, and it might even change how you think about poetry. What do you think?"

"Let's do it—dinner, I mean. And I'll look into the poetry thing too. That's a great idea. Two great ideas, in fact."

Alex looked as happy as if he had found a solution to an intricate puzzle.

I worried about what to serve for dinner. What kind of food did they like? What would they expect? What were the wrong choices? How could I avoid offending them? I think I chose at least a dozen menus—and then rejected each and every one of them—too white, too black, too bland, too nothing, too frivolous and irrelevant. Trying too hard. Not trying enough. I felt awkward, clueless, stupid. A total crisis of confidence. Out of my depth. I so wanted to make a good impression, to recover from my years, decades even, of neglect and ignorance, all in one perfect dinner with one perfect black couple.

I can now see that I put way too much weight on that single meal, on the food I would serve at that single meal—it was totally ridiculous, pathetic, laughable. But I also have to admit that at the time it felt like I was preparing for a momentous state dinner. And that I had totally lost my sense of perspective and proportion, not to mention my sense of humor.

And then, my problem vanished when the new professor and his wife said why not meet at a restaurant, which they chose, probably without any qualms at all about what Alex and I might like. It was a Thai restaurant on Solano, good food, not expensive, small enough that we could talk easily. A perfect choice.

They were an attractive couple, young—maybe late thirties or early forties, no children. She was a person of paler color than he was. They both dressed with an East Coast formality and they gleamed as if they were cloaked in shiny corporate shells, although she was an eye surgeon, not a senior executive. Over skewers of chicken satay and plates of pad thai and pumpkin curry, they chatted about houses and house prices and the home they were renovating in the Berkeley Hills—how a view of the Bay added 'at least a hundred thou' to the price of a house up there. The husband talked about the exciting research frontiers in psycholinguistics, and how he hoped to bridge the barriers that separated the psycholinguists from the sociolinguists. Alex tried to insert poetry into the barrier-bridging, but he was ignored.

When we started on the second bottle of wine, I tried to talk about Hurricane Katrina, but beyond a shaking of heads and a 'dreadful' and a 'terrible,' the topic died. The professor was more interested in talking about the miserable Boston winters that he was so happy to leave behind. "Snow up to here," he said, holding his hand to his waist. "And the next year, up to here," moving his hand up to his chest. "It just kept getting worse." The eye surgeon's eyes tightened as he said this, suggesting that she didn't agree, but she had been mostly silent for some time, so it was hard to be sure. I suspected marital discord, that she hadn't wanted to leave Boston, although it could just as easily have been the stress of moving across the country and new jobs and moving into an expensive house that needed immediate renovations.

They both thanked Alex for the meal and the personal welcome to Berkeley. The eye surgeon said how nice it was to meet someone that her husband would be working with. Neither of them said a word about getting together again, and I realized that the restaurant suggestion had been their way of avoiding the obligation ever to invite us to their home in the hills with the view of the bay. We had simply bounced off their shiny defensive facade and ricocheted back into our own life.

"Pleasant-enough people—obviously very smart," I said to Alex as we walked home.

"Although maybe not a big help with your project," he said. "I imagine we look so old to them that they can't imagine either one of us being anything but boring."

"Not a hypothesis they bothered to test—I can't remember them asking either of us a single question."

"You know that psychologists call that confirmation bias, don't you?"

We laughed. And I told him about that long-ago dinner with you and Brown, also in an ethnic restaurant, and how badly that one had gone, how the two of you had instantly concluded that Finn and I were not the kind of people you wanted to be seen with. How Finn and I had never talked about it, how we had never been able to laugh it off.

When Alex and I got home we had another glass of wine just for the fun of it. We sat in our swivel chairs and looked out our bay window—a bay window with no view of the bay—at the garden and the houses beyond it and the western sky above the trees. And talked and talked for a long time, watching the bright lights of airplanes cross the night sky.

The course in Afro-American poetry turned out to be much more useful. The professor was passionate, the students engaged, and the poetry itself searing and honest and raw and beautiful. Often it had a didactic edge that had disappeared long ago from other—I guess I mean white—poems. I was struck with how insistently these poems needed to communicate, to connect, with readers and listeners. Especially listeners—much of it needed to be heard, rather than read, so that the listener could experience the way the poem assaulted the ears with anger and honesty and compelling rhythms.

My favorite discovery was June Jordan's poetry. She touched every nerve in my body with lines like this:

> . . . I have been wrong the wrong sex the wrong age
> the wrong skin the wrong nose the wrong hair the
> wrong need the wrong dream . . .
> *I am not wrong: Wrong is not my name*

I felt I had no right to find my own life in those lines, although I did. As I did again, years later, when I read Claudia Rankine's poem that starts *The world is wrong.* The best black poetry always makes me think that somehow, when the poet's skin is the color of the words, not the page, their words have more impact. Sometimes those black words punch you right in the face.

In the classroom I always sat in a far corner. I liked watching the young students, mostly black and female, liked trying to guess which poems they would engage with. I thought about moving forward, getting more involved, but I didn't think they'd be interested in what a grey-haired woman had to say—a woman who suddenly felt so white and so old, who was only auditing the course, who had neither lived the context of these poems nor known anyone who had. The few other white students, although less than half my age, also tended to migrate towards the margins of the room and mostly took diligent notes, rather than inject themselves into the discussions. It was as though, despite the professor's meticulous even-handedness, we had unconsciously absorbed what it means to be a minority—we positioned our bodies so they would fade into the background, we silenced our voices, we became quietly deferential and observant. We ceded the space to the dominant majority and they occupied it as unquestioningly as white males in a boardroom.

It was the day the professor pointed out that June Jordan's lines resonated because they were at the same time so specific to one person and so universal—the day my feelings about the poem felt vindicated rather than presumptuous—that I stayed behind after class to talk with her. Which is how I learned that Jordan had taught at Berkeley until she had died of breast cancer a few years earlier. And I had been oblivious. "You would have liked her," the professor said. "She wanted everyone to write poetry."

That evening I inflicted my frustration on the broccoli I was chopping for dinner. I was angry that I had once again missed out. All my life, ever since I was a kid, the interesting things always happened somewhere else—and even though I had been here for all those years, practically within walking distance of June Jordan, I missed out anyhow. For all I knew we had the same oncologist, we might have sat across from each other in her waiting room, oblivious within the cocoon of our own fears and problems. And then she was dead.

I never returned to my Hurricane Katrina poem, although I went on to audit an African-American history course as well. The more I learned, the more I realized it wasn't my poem to write—those courses made me a little more knowledgeable about people of color, but not nearly enough to write about their experience.

Neither did I retreat back into my ignorance, though—Ardith and I started going to Poetry 4 the People events in Berkeley and Oakland, where the organizers sometimes read one of June Jordan's poems to honor the woman who had founded the group in the years before she died. We also heard new poems by new poets in an eclectic cacophony of creativity and purpose—and we were able to witness and applaud their efforts. After a while, black poets would sometimes offer us a seat at their table.

The generous atmosphere I felt in those encounters—a casual, no-big-deal acceptance—made it easy to buy into the notion that the country was truly on the verge of becoming post-racial. After all, as Ardith and I said to each other when we helped elect America's first black President, it's about time. We were as giddy as all those beautiful young people who gathered in Chicago to celebrate Obama's victory. How could anyone not be caught up in the hope of that moment? How could anyone not imagine that a post-racial future was possible, was worth working toward? That moment felt like the actual achievement of the promise we had recited since childhood: *One nation, under God, with liberty and justice for all.*

But of course that moment coincided with the depths of the great financial crisis that threatened to topple the mega-banks like dominoes. So instead of change for the better things got worse. Over the next year or two or three, more and more people lost their homes and their jobs and their futures to rampant fraud. Not that anyone ever went to jail, which is something that must give you hope in your current situation. Instead, the bankers and the lawyers who created the crisis got richer by hollowing out the middle class and making more people poor. They saved the banks, though. And all the experts said that if they hadn't, things would have been far worse. It all makes your troubles pale in comparison, don't you think? Maybe no one will make a movie about your disgrace.

Anyhow, I never heard your opinions on the crisis because by then Fox News had younger women on air. They must have kicked you upstairs, or sidelined you, or streamlined the organization, or reorganized their strategic priorities, or all of the above. Which was probably just as well, since you had never had a head for numbers, not even in high school, long before you counted bodies that weren't there in New Orleans.

Plus, the year the great recession started was also the year we both turned sixty. I'm guessing that was also the year that your cheeks gave birth to tiny baby jowls—maybe exactly at the same time as Joy gave birth to tiny Maggie and I became a grandmother. Did she really name her baby after Margaret Thatcher? I couldn't ask. I didn't want to know. I just held the child and cooed maggie-maggie-maggie-maggie over and over again, to disconnect her from that demented old woman. And to banish your triumphant smile from my mind. At least she didn't name the baby after you, I thought, and it was a comfort.

In any event, both young Maggie and your jowls thrived—not at all like the sickly, anemic economy. We can assume that you weren't paying attention to your burgeoning jowls, so what were you doing during that time? You didn't have a daughter to worry about, a daughter who threw herself into yoga to get her figure back and into work to get her career back on track. Nor a son-in-law who radiated blissful contentment with his daughter strapped to his chest in her Baby Bjorn.

I don't imagine anyone foreclosed on your mortgage, if you still had one. But maybe your retirement funds sagged, like mine and Alex's did. Maybe it was helpful to have those lucrative corporate board appointments when those big paychecks from Fox stopped showing up in your bank account. That might explain why you cozied up to those pharmaceutical firms, finding ever more clever ways for them to make money from charitable donations. Or maybe you too were seduced by the real estate bubble, borrowing and investing and over-extending your finances, just like all those other poor suckers. Maybe you should write a second volume of your autobiography. You could fill us in on all the things we don't know.

A nickel ain't worth a dime anymore. —*Yogi Berra*

FRIDAY NIGHT: New York City

There you sit, drinking your second—or is it already your third?—bourbon. You're in your favorite chair, feet up on the ottoman that you brought back from Turkey all those years ago. It helps that your cat purrs in your lap. She's a Russian Blue, with luxurious fur that finds its way onto your clothes and into every nook of your apartment. But it's worth it, because you love digging your fingers into that softness and massaging the muscles underneath.

She's old now, poor Cobalt. You thought you were naming her after a paint color, but then it turned out that Cobalt was the name of a CIA torture site in Afghanistan. One of life's ironies, that her name turned out to have political overtones. Was it the Turkish ambassador who did a double-take when he heard her name? You can't remember anymore, although you can still recall startled eyebrows and a bearded head swivelling toward you when he overheard her name.

Your chair faces the blank television, because if you actually hear what they're saying about you it will only keep you up all night. Instead, with the help of your bourbon and your blue cat, you can sustain the tiny hope that something else has happened, that the world has moved on, that you're—possibly, hopefully—home free.

What would it take to get your name out of the headlines? The most obvious is a terrorist attack, but only if it was unexpected. Another suicide bomber in one of the usual war-torn countries wouldn't be enough, since your virtual American blood is still more interesting than actual gore in the Middle East or Africa. But real American blood—for instance, yet another dead African-American, especially if he were killed by police—that would work. It would be nonstop analysis and arguments and hand-wringing about Black Lives Matter vs. Blue Lives Matter, with a side order of historical perspective and another of what this bodes for the future.

You contemplate turning on the television, just to see whether something terrible has already happened. But it doesn't matter enough, not this minute, not while you have the comfort of Cobalt under your fingertips. Soon, when the cat has had enough stroking, you'll go to bed. The rest can wait.

> I pledge allegiance / to the flag:
> *a pleasure region / new thing lad* — *Michael Magee*

FRIDAY EVENING: Berkeley, CA

They're all gathered on the deck, wine glasses in hand, sitting in mismatched chairs around the fire pit, enjoying its warmth as the sun sinks lower in the sky. The sunset is glorious, drawing attention away from the parched, neglected garden.

Max has finished telling his story of last night's awards dinner, where they gave him a lifetime achievement award. "They give them out like Crackerjacks—it's their way of telling you that your life's work is over," he says. Sarah sighs, the exact same sound his first wife made when he told his stories.

The rest of them, Joy and Liam, Ardith, Alex and Michelle, make more appreciative comments. Maggie runs out with a fistful of markers and paper and sets to work at one of the small tables.

Michelle: Speaking of careers coming to an end, what do you think of the Cynthia Lord story?

Alex: Michelle's been gloating over her problems all day, if you can believe it.

Ardith: Of course she has—so have I—don't you love it when the rich and famous get their comeuppance?

Michelle: Is that a word anyone even uses anymore?

Max: The whole thing is pure theatre.

Joy: Maybe for your generation. To me it's just some random story that grew because it was a slow news day. By next week something else will be trending on Twitter.

Max: You're right, but it's still good theatre while it lasts.

Ardith: So are you saying that she won't get her comeuppance?

Alex: Could someone explain it to me? I just don't get it—why is everyone so interested in this? More wine, anyone?

Michelle: Since she used to be my friend, I'll say that I think it's because it's important—because it's a perfect metaphor for what's been going wrong with the country. We need to see—we need for Maggie and all her friends to see—that lying and fraud and all the rest—are wrong, even if you're rich. Especially if you're rich.

Ardith: Max—you're an oncologist. How does it make you feel when she pretends she has cancer?

Max: I'm not on the hook—I'm officially retired. I don't have to be an expert anymore. But yeah, that whole fake cancer thing is going to hurt the Cancer Foundation. I'd love some wine, Alex.

Joy: I don't think they need to worry. If they're smart they'll throw her off the board—they probably already have—and then they'll switch their focus to childhood cancers or something else that's worlds away from whatever cancer she had. In a couple of months Cynthia Lord and all her problems won't even be history, because everybody forgets everything these days.

Liam: That sounds pretty cynical even for you.

Joy: We live in cynical times, dear, in case you hadn't noticed.

Michelle: But it is a metaphor—she's a metaphor. Hard work and merit are for suckers—these days to get rich you just have to be dirty. And that's why I think the story goes beyond just a news cycle. Especially if they indict her, of course.

Joy: Right. Like that will happen. What do you think, Sarah?

Sarah: I think I'd like some more wine.

Max: You've known her all your life, Michelle—why does she bother you so much?

And that's all she needs. Michelle regales them with the story of Cynthia's youthful crimes, the way she treated people at NPR, her convenient shift to the political right that enabled her climb to fame and fortune—she inserts a few words about her skills as an interviewer, maybe to demonstrate her objectivity—and ends with Cynthia's self-serving racism during the Katrina fiasco.

The story receives a warm reception—attention, laughter, and animated speculation about Cynthia's supposed crimes.

Sarah has avoided sighing since Michelle started talking, although she hasn't been listening either. Instead she takes a sip from her glass and watches Maggie cram two more crab and avocado toasts into her mouth, green muck smeared on face and fingers. She has to wonder how anyone can like children. She will not engage. Not my problem, she thinks. Instead she turns to Ardith with a vague smile. "How long have you known Michelle and Alex?"

Ardith responds with a long story that involves poetry and, bizarrely, the Challenger explosion, but Sarah isn't really listening. There's no exam at the end of this encounter. She monitors the tone, though, and when Ardith's story starts to slow down, she inserts some encouraging noises. The longer she talks, the less effort she has to make. It works. Ardith tells her about Michelle's cancer, and then Michelle's mother's cancer, and how she herself had a cancer scare not too long ago. More encouraging noises. More story from Ardith.

She'll be back home in a few days and that's it until next year. She gives Ardith her best smile and says, "That is so interesting! But tell me all about your poetry—and where can I buy one of your books?"

Max is not only having far more fun than his wife, he's aware of it too, which makes him feel a little guilty, but it's a guilty pleasure, something that adds to his enjoyment of this evening. This is special. The last day of winter, and he's sitting outside with a glass of wine, far from the dreariness of March on the East Coast. And he's still zinging with the pleasure of last night's award. Sarah will get over it—all of it. It looks like she's at least enjoying the wine—she should—it's very good.

There's something about seeing his sister that always makes him feel younger. Not that she's looking particularly young anymore. The cancer all those years ago took its toll—her hair is colorless, her skin wrinkled, even the way she moves looks old. He would have spared her all that if he could. Nevertheless, maybe because of her absurdly youthful insistence on justice—the idea makes him laugh, which he disguises as a cough—the overall effect, at least for him, is young.

Or maybe he's mixing up Michelle and Joy in his mind. Joy looks so much like Michelle used to—the same quick smile, the same energy, although as far as he can tell Joy is far more comfortable in her own skin than his sister ever was. Probably Finn's fault. Not that he ever really knew the man. What he remembers is his instant dislike. Finn's beard was off-putting, his arrogance even more so. Thank God she left him. Alex suits her better in every way—if he's honest about it, the two of them are better together than he and Sarah will ever be. The liberal hopey-changey stuff actually works for them. He coughs again, eliciting a look of concern from Joy, which he deflects with a new topic.

"So, tell me all about what's happening in Silicon Valley. When is the IPO happening, so I can buy some stock?"

Liam sees the delighted smile Joy gives her uncle and can tell immediately that he has asked about her work. The right-wing capitalists of the family, ready to have multiple orgasms over stock options and the uncountable riches of an IPO. Her single-minded focus on money irks him. As does the expensive wine she insisted on bringing—in its own portable wine cooler that she spent half an hour searching all over the house for, as if a bag of ice wouldn't have worked perfectly well. And the over-the-top cake from the special bakery.

He swallows some wine and focuses on Maggie. "That is one gnarly dinosaur there, sweetie." She rewards him with a grin.

Michelle and Alex retreat to the kitchen to dress the salad and cook the pasta.

"What's going on with Joy and Liam? They've done nothing but snipe at each other." Alex has his back to the deck and keeps his voice low.

"Or ignore each other. I was wondering too. Do you think I should talk to her?" A frown creases her forehead, but she masks her worry with vigorous tossing of the salad.

"Probably not the best time."

"It could just be her work—she's been putting in crazy hours. That's got to be tough on Liam—and Maggie too. Here—can you put this on the table?"

"What else can I do?"

"Open some more wine—and slice some bread. How about if we keep Maggie for the weekend? Give them some time by themselves?"

"Let's do it—good idea. That way they won't have to leave early to get her to bed."

Michelle's frown fades. "I'm not sure Sarah is very happy with Max right now either—should we keep her too?"

Alex shakes his head, vehemently. "Please don't get involved in that one. Definitely not our problem."

The sun is setting, the temperature dropping—everyone moves inside, taking wineglasses and various threads of conversations with them. They crowd around a dining room table better suited to six than eight. The table is a jumble of place settings, two enormous bowls of pasta, a salad, an assortment of tall and short candles, and Sarah's big bouquet of flowers.

Max takes the initiative. "The flowers are gorgeous, but do you mind if I move them? That way we can all see each other." They're already on the sideboard before anyone can say anything. He does not look at his wife. Nor does she look at him. Other people jostle for chairs, change the subject, say that the food looks and smells delicious. The moment passes.

Michelle: Max, do you remember how Dad always used to tell you that you could grow up to be President? Did it ever make you think about getting into politics?

Max: He should have said it to you—you would make a much better President—although I'm not sure that's a really big compliment given how bad I would be. Anyhow, there was one time when I stuck my toe in the political waters. It's not a bad story. The Democrats in Massachusetts were doing some really dumb stuff—I don't remember what, but at the time it made me angry—so I wrote a letter to the editor. The next thing I know I get a phone call from a local Republican who wants me to get involved. He invites me to a Fourth of July barbecue, says I would enjoy meeting people who agree with me. So we went—Lisa and I—this was just before she got sick— maybe that's why I remember it so clearly. I also remember Lisa warning me not to go, as if she had some premonition that we didn't have much time, but I said, 'It's just a barbecue—let's see what it's like' and so we went. And met the most aggressive group of power-hungry self-promoters I've ever had the misfortune to spend time with. There was not a word about what might be good for Massachusetts, no one pretended to be interested in policy or public service—just what's in it for me—and for you, if you only join us. The whole thing was nudge-nudge wink-wink—we both had showers when we got home.

Michelle: Interesting that you said 'a toe in the water'—most of you was still on the outside, so that you could see the water was dirty, unlike the rest of the people there. And then saying you needed a shower, extending the water metaphor—maybe you should be writing poetry? It reminds me of Yeats: *The blood-dimmed tide is loosed, and everywhere / The ceremony of innocence is drowned; / The best lack all conviction, while the worst / Are full of passionate intensity.*

Max: That's funny—and you're right, they were definitely full of passionate intensity. About all the wrong things.

Michelle: So why do you still vote Republican?

Max: I don't really believe it makes any difference at all, except that we need a change every few years. Or maybe I'm an eternal optimist that believes Republicans will govern less badly than Democrats, at least in Massachusetts. But believe me, they're all sleazy.

Liam: You sound almost as cynical as Joy.

Joy: I only do it as a balance to the irresponsible left-wing utopia you dream about. Someone has to be a realist.

Alex steers the conversation back to Yeats and metaphor. Michelle distracts Joy with a question about summer travel plans, which engages Sarah as well. Ardith watches with admiration as Liam and Joy's argument shrivels from neglect.

Max: It shouldn't just be water or Cynthia—how about me? I should be a metaphor too. An oncologist whose parents both died of cancer, whose wife died of cancer? That seems like a ready-made metaphor to me.

Michelle: That's not quite a metaphor—maybe a metathree, though—I'll need to think about that.

Max: Are you saying I have to die of cancer too if I want to be a metaphor? That doesn't sound fair.

Michelle: Or it could be me—that's more likely. But no, it's not fair. Ask Alex—he's always telling me life isn't fair.

Alex: So what makes Cynthia a metaphor, while poor Max only rates a metathree?

Ardith: Metaphors need more nuance, more contradiction even, don't you think? Look at Max—oncologist plus three cancer deaths. Ironic, yes, but no subtleties or shades of meaning. Whereas with Cynthia we have big themes like fame turning into infamy—trust betrayed—and the cancer / fake cancer thing just underlines how America is betraying so many people.

Joy: Wow, that's a farfetched analysis—I thought it was just about our love of juicy gossip—although when there's no sex—when it's just about money—it's not all that great as gossip either.

Michelle: There's power too—don't forget power.

Sarah: I need some more wine, Alex.

Alex feels sorry for Sarah, although he doesn't translate that into a big pour. She's had a lot of wine already. He can tell that she hates these kinds of word games, where ideas collide and ricochet and create unlikely connections. She was happier comparing travel plans, until Joy deserted her.

Joy, though—Joy looks, finally, like she's having fun. And Michelle and Max are too.

Liam has retreated, focusing his attention on Maggie. The two of them are talking about dinosaurs, which gives Alex an opening to ask about keeping Maggie for the weekend and taking her to see dinosaurs at the campus museum. They both beam at him as though he's the best grandfather in the world.

Max: You were saying earlier, about Cynthia Lord turning into a right wing racist—how do you think that happened?

Michelle: It feels like it was the whole country, or most of it, and she went along for the ride because it was the easiest, fastest way to get ahead. Looking back, I don't think she was ever committed to anything except herself. So in her twenties she used Brown to display her radical chic—but when radical wasn't chic anymore she happily adopted the next new thing, which—unfortunately—was the rising Republican party, which itself was also becoming increasingly racist. Helped by the get-rich-at-all-costs mindset that went with it.

Joy: Don't you think that's kind of simplistic? I mean lots of people—especially as we get older and more experienced—stop expecting governments to fix everything. And they get fed up with government squandering tax dollars on useless projects.

Liam: But it's not just the less-government stuff—the more interesting thing is the racism. How do you go from having a black lover to becoming a blatant racist?

Max: Hey, Cynthia may have done a lot of things wrong, but no one's accusing her of killing unarmed black people.

Liam: If Michelle's right, the kinds of things Cynthia was saying during Katrina are the kinds of things that set the tone—they encourage cops to shoot fast because they're scared for their own lives. Alex, how does someone make that kind of leap?

Alex: What I think is that, when you're part of a system—in Cynthia's case that would be the media world, but it also applies to cops on the job or any of us when we're embedded in a larger group—we gain status when we reflect the group norms. Cynthia, like so many successful people, is a very good chameleon—so good she probably does it without thinking. When she's swimming in racist waters she reflects racist attitudes.

Ardith: Maybe we've overworked the water metaphor? I mean, it's all about money, isn't it? Whether we talk about Cynthia Lord or Wall Street greed or elections or the price of tea, when you get to the root of it, it's always money money money."

Michelle: The price of tea?

Alex: No, let's talk about this. What is it about money—why is it so central to everything? Money could be the most pervasive metaphor in America. Way more than water, although I may have spent too much time with poets. Max, how do you think about money?

Max: Okay, money. For me it's how we keep score—successful

people have more of it and losers have less of it. If you have it, it means vacations and golf and nice cars. Whether that's a metaphor or not, I don't know, but that's what it means to me.

Ardith: I'm tempted to say money is the root of all evil, but that's such a cliché that I refuse to use it.

Michelle: You just did.

Ardith: Moving right along—yes, another cliché—money is what I have to worry about when I'd rather be doing almost anything else. Rent, food, books—they all require money. Money is a boring necessity that gets in the way of all the things that give my life meaning. If you lose track of it you can get yourself in trouble and then you waste even more time and effort trying to get it straightened out. There's a terrific poem by Harryette Mullen—I think it's called *Black Nikes*. Anyhow, in it she says people are *'Noiseless patient spiders / paid with dirt when what we want is star dust.'* Money is dirt—I agree with that. Although I'm not sure that I'm a particularly patient spider. What about you, Michelle?

Michelle: I like that poem too. But much as I love metaphors, I'm not sure about money being dirt. For me money has been important mostly when I didn't have enough—like when Joy was young and a broken hot water heater was a minor catastrophe. But I was also proud of myself when I found creative ways to spend less, whether it was getting Joy to think of lentil soup as a special treat or finding free things to do with her on weekends. So for me money is complicated—I think it imposes restraints that we need, that it makes us think about what our priorities are, what we value, what we can substitute for money—all of which is good. But when money takes over a person's life, because they always have too little—or if they're always greedy for more—then it warps the humanity in us and makes us less than what we could be. So, a two edged sword? Because I can do clichés just as well as Ardith?

Liam: When I think about money I think about income disparity—the way a few people at the top of the pyramid have more money than they could spend in a million lifetimes while twenty percent of our children live in poverty—that's one out of every five children. In the richest country in the world. In 2015. Unbelievable.

Joy: My, aren't we getting earnest. I'll just say money is what it is.

Your turn, Maggie—what does money mean to you?

Maggie: I think money is magic, because you can turn it into anything you want.

The conversation splinters again under the combined weight of Joy's sneer and Maggie's fairytale vision. Liam looks embarrassed, although Ardith is coaxing him into talking about Maggie's school. Alex would apologize to him if he could. The last thing he wanted was to aggravate whatever is going on between him and Joy.

It's later now. Joy's cake has been demolished, with much appreciation. Maggie has said goodnight to everyone and gone to bed to dream of dinosaurs. And yet no one is quite ready to leave. Max, because he knows he won't see his sister or niece again for another year. Joy and Liam, because they have a long drive back to Mountain View without the counterweight of their daughter in the back seat. And Ardith, because she wants to find out what happens next. Sarah could, with a simple sentence—'it's getting late,' or 'thank you for a wonderful evening'—precipitate everyone toward the door, but she no longer cares when the evening ends. There's still some wine on the table, and its proximity is more enticing than the prospect of getting out of her chair, going through the niceties of saying goodnight, and walking to the car. So she pours the rest of the bottle into her glass.

And then Max says, "Why don't we move back outside by the fire pit? It would be lovely to sit outside and watch the last day of winter end."

Michelle offers to make coffee. Max volunteers to help. Alex roots out some jackets and sweaters, then restarts the fire. People rearrange themselves: Joy tucks her feet up and curls under a jacket, looking tired but more relaxed than she has all evening. Sarah stretches her feet toward the warmth. Liam, next to Sarah, hunches forward toward the fire, as if he can see his thoughts in the flames. Ardith settles into the most comfortable chair with a small sound of contentment, her eyes bright with expectation, while Alex, still standing, looks toward the kitchen, willing Michelle and Max to hurry and join them as the silence stretches toward discomfort. To fill the void, he talks about the first thing he thinks of: how he likes to watch the bright lights of the airplanes crossing the dark sky, and how he imagines the passengers looking forward to arriving home. Sarah responds, and the conversation meanders around departures and homecomings.

In the kitchen Max and Michelle work side-by-side, also not talking. Max is engaged in an internal argument, trying to decide whether to tell his sister about how, back in the day, he had once had sex with Cynthia. It's a good story, although he's never told it to anyone. Would she appreciate it, given how she feels about Cynthia?

He can still picture her, that day at the beach—her perfect body with all its touch-me curves, the pale blue bikini, the dark red hair that looked better than any shampoo ad he'd ever seen. And hear her, the way she said yes when he offered her an ice cream cone, and then a soft yes to his kiss in the woods beyond the beach, and a quieter yes as they lay down together. And then, that strange inertia that seemed to come over her when he touched those curves, not moving into his touch but not pulling away either. She was only the second girl he'd had sex with. And he was so painfully young—if he had been thinking at all it must have been about his own urgency, his own pleasure. But it was an empty act, something felt off about it even at the time, not that he could put his finger on how, or why. What he remembers most was afterwards, how whenever Cynthia looked at him, he felt like he had taken part in a lab experiment.

No. He makes up his mind. Whether for her sake or his own or even Cynthia's, he's not going to share his story. It doesn't really matter why. He will remain the old fool that he is instead of becoming a bigger one—he'll keep his secret to himself. Unless she were to ask, in which case he would tell her, maybe, and maybe it would make her laugh. Or not. There's the rub. He muffles a laugh, but not enough.

"What's funny?"

"I was just thinking how much I like being here. I wonder if I could convince Sarah to move." He doesn't wait for a response, though. He picks up the tray of coffee mugs and heads out the door.

Alex is relieved to see them come out. Now the conversation will hopefully move back to something with some substance—or at least some humor. Interesting, he thinks, how one or two people can be crucial to the mood of a gathering. What's needed is someone with passion. Like Michelle—whether she's obsessing about Cynthia Lord or longing for people to be better than they are, or best of all, insisting that poetry needs to matter, she gives the gift of passion. Unlike Sarah, now rejecting the coffee. He can't remember ever seeing her really interested in anything—certainly not tonight, unless you count the wine. But of course he only sees Sarah when he himself is around, and he's guessing that she doesn't like anyone in Max's family very much. She may be—she must be—different when she isn't here. Otherwise why did Max ever marry her?

Although Max doesn't have a lot of passion either—he just has more personality than his wife. And he doesn't take life particularly seriously. Probably a defensive mechanism—oncologists see a lot of people die.

And the rest of them? Ardith—yes, although not as intense as Michelle. Ardith is passionate about poetry and language and words, but also strong colors, whether in clothing or art or nature. And good food.

Joy? Her job and her daughter, both uncomplicated loves. Mid-century modern. Motorcycles. Expensive things that reflect her good taste. Liam used to belong on that list, but somehow that's changing, and not for the better. He thinks back to their last dinner in Mountain View, how every time Joy said anything about her work Liam turned to talk to Maggie. And how, when asked about his own work, all he said was 'a lot of frustrating politics—not worth talking about.'

To Alex's surprise, it's not Michelle but Joy who initiates a new topic. "What about Cynthia Lord's marriage, Mom? Did you know much about it?"

Michelle: Not really. But right around the time that Reagan was elected, out of the blue she married her cameraman. I forget his name, but he was good-looking in that bland, Republican kind of way. Her Christmas card was a picture of the two of them on horseback with snowy peaks in the background. Anyhow, because of her previous relationship with Brown, I thought of her new husband as Pink. But a few years later her Christmas cards started arriving with pictures of just her and her cat. Plus—and I love this—something with leopard spots in every picture. A blouse or a cushion or a painting of a leopard. And always her red fingernails, which seemed to get longer every year. She'd clearly transferred her affections from her cameraman to red nails and big, predatory cats.

Ardith: Isn't Pink a great name, though? And do you remember we invented other names, like Ebony for Brown's wife?

Michelle: If only she'd married again—we could have called the next one Ecru—an upper-crust beige, with a hint of crudity—just the right kind of guy for Cynthia, don't you think?

Even Sarah is laughing. But Joy isn't finished. "Why do you think they split up?"

Michelle: My guess would be that she discovered that she didn't have room for someone in her life who couldn't enhance her public image. But that's probably my snarkiness speaking.

Liam: There has to be more to it than that when a marriage goes wrong, doesn't there? It's not like throwing out a book that you end up not liking. How did things go wrong with you and Finn?

Michelle: In general I'd have to say ending a marriage is more like throwing out a chicken that's gone bad. But no specifics—I haven't had enough to drink for that—and especially not in front of my daughter.

Joy: Don't avoid the question on my account. Or I'll have to tell my version.

Ardith: If I know your mother, you can't bully her into telling, so you might as well go ahead.

Joy: I was just a kid, but looking back I have to think that all those students that Dad brought into the house after we moved here had something to do with it. I wonder if it was the same with Cynthia—whether her husband went looking for younger women too.

Ardith: You could be right—I can't imagine Cynthia putting up with that. But that begs the question—why did she marry him in the first place? How could the chicken smell wonderful just before it smelled so bad?

Michelle: Here we go with over-extended metaphors again. Marriages fail—it happens all the time, and I doubt that there's ever a clear line from a single cause to a single effect. As far as I can tell, when the chicken goes off, both people are responsible—from the hope that went into buying it in the first place, to letting themselves get distracted and failing to put it in the fridge, to not caring enough to cook it and serve it, to breaking the domestic cycle that includes sharing dinners together. So I can imagine Cynthia and Pink losing that connection and then not bothering to reconnect. Her fault? His fault? In the end, their fault—or no one's.

Joy: At least they didn't have any children. Although even for children divorce isn't all bad—I think more than anything else it taught me good management skills.

Alex: Seriously? I've never heard that before.

Joy: Absolutely. I think it had to do with my need to regain some sort of control over my environment after the split—I still remember that sense of having zero control, that things were being done to me without anyone even asking me what I thought—it all felt awful. Even this house—mom bought it before I even knew we were moving, it was a done deal—and it was hate at first sight. Thank god, Alex, that you came into her life and the renovation finally got rid of that horrid old-people smell.

Alex: Watch out—we're getting older and it might come back. But get back to management skills—I'm intrigued.

Joy: Like I said, it came down to getting control. For instance, my dad would bring home these young women, and they would all have these ideas about how to deal with me. The worst were the ones who decided they should be my mother, but others would pretend to be my friend. So I had to figure out how to convince them to go away. The wannabe mothers were the easiest—the more they tried to change my behavior, the worse I behaved. They couldn't stand it. So, gone. The friendly ones I could get to buy me stuff or let me play with their makeup, so they weren't as bad, but if they started to get serious, I'd push them away—I'd be clingy with my dad, or tell them things about dad that I knew they wouldn't like, or if nothing else worked, I'd scream in the middle of the night and say I was having nightmares. Not what they signed up for, so gone again. It was the ones who ignored me who lasted the longest, especially if they kept away from my dad when I was around. What I learned was that when you commit to a goal and a decent plan, with alternatives if necessary, you can make almost anything happen.

Liam slips away from the conversation and seeks out the privacy of the bathroom, where he leans over the sink, head down, unable to look himself in the face. He can't believe what he's just heard. Joy convincing herself that divorce is a great way to learn management skills. So Maggie's about to get a crash course that will presumably prepare her for a successful future. When was she planning on sharing the news with him? Or did she actually intend to inform him as part of a general announcement? Why? To prevent insider trading? Not funny. He flushes the toilet and washes his hands, in case anyone is listening. To hell with the drought. He dries his hands carefully, decides that he will insist on custody.

Back outside, he drags his chair farther into the gloom. At least the conversation has shifted again, away from the growth opportunities of divorce to something more in keeping with his mood.

Michelle: We've made a mess of everything, haven't we? We didn't mean to, but we did. Just like Philip Larkin said about parents, but we did it to everything.

Max: I think you're looking through the wrong end of the telescope. Things are never going to be perfect—they can't be, we're just human—but look at us—I don't see a lot of suffering humanity.

Alex: But it's not just about us, Max. I think what Michelle's getting at is that we've collectively lost balance. Back when we were young, society was supported by three competing institutions—we had corporations to make things and create wealth, we had unions that forced the corporations to share the wealth, and we had governments that created rules to keep us honest. More or less, anyhow, but it was all enough to make us feel that the future was going to be better than the present. Since then, though, over the past thirty or forty years, under the banner of globalization we first got rid of unions, especially in the private sector, and then we weakened governments through tax cuts until they became pretty much dysfunctional. So now the only real power left is corporate power, and there's nothing left to make them share. So the future looks bleaker than the present.

Ardith: And that's why California is running out of water and nobody's doing much of anything about global warming—and why the income disparity Liam was talking about is getting worse and worse. And race relations are an oxymoron—except for violent confrontations, it feels like black America and white America are two different planets.

Max: Whoa, you're all ganging up on me here—and throwing out more flabby progressive notions than my poor brain can process all at once.

Joy: Can I help you fight off the flabby progressives? It'll be fun—where do you want to start?

Flabby progressives? Liam knows Alex was saying something important. Does she really need to turn everything they're talking about into a joke? He's irritated by his wife's frivolous attitude—and by her inane giggle. But not surprised. What he doesn't understand, what he can't get his mind around, is how or when their marriage turned into the same kind of oxymoron as Ardith's race relations. What was he doing instead of paying attention? He wants to object, he wants to scream his outrage. He wants to force her to remember that she used to love him, progressive notions and all. But he wants custody more. He swallows his coffee and drowns his words.

Joy saw Liam yank his chair away from the fire, and now she sees him drink his coffee as if it's poison. Why can't he lighten up? Something's bothering him, and although she's not sure what, whatever it is seems to be getting worse. He's been so humorless all evening—practically turgid, except when he was talking to Maggie. And he hardly ate or drank anything, even though he loves pasta. Could he be depressed? Is he jealous that she has the better job? She decides not to think about it, not now, and turns back to Max. "So, who do you think will run against Hillary?"

Max: Interesting you should ask. I saw just yesterday—maybe in *The Guardian*?—that Trump is opening a campaign office in New Hampshire.

Michelle: Wait a minute—you read *The Guardian*?

Max: Don't get your hopes up—I'm not changing my stripes.

Somebody at the conference had a copy. But I thought it was interesting about Trump—especially since the Republicans don't have anyone yet who looks like a winner.

Michelle: There's no way he's serious, though. He's been talking about running for what, twenty years? And he's never followed through.

Alex: My money's on Scott Walker.

Max: Not so fast—you have to remember that Trump's getting older—this is his last chance. And the whole country is disgusted with politicians.

Joy: I have to say, it could be interesting—the battle of the blondes—that sounds like politics and a reality show all rolled into one.

Sarah: What this country really needs is a shift to a younger generation. Clinton and the lot of them should be put out to pasture.

Ardith: But he's a joke, isn't he? Please tell me he's a joke.

Michelle: Nothing to worry about—trust me—even Republicans aren't that dumb.

The election talk leaves Ardith feeling abruptly tired and discouraged. Or is it watching Joy and Liam at odds with each other? There's a poem hidden in this evening, a narrative poem about hope and its opposite. Tomorrow she'll work on it. Right now she's not even sure why it's a narrative poem, although she knows in her aching bones that it is. "I guess it's time for me to head home—unless somebody still has some juicy Cynthia gossip to share, of course." She smiles, pushes herself out of her low chair with less grace than she would like, then adjusts her scarf to give her hip time to recover.

The others get to their feet as well, make offers to help clean up that Michelle deflects, saying most of it is already done. Max tries to insist, but Alex distracts him by inviting him to join them tomorrow to go see the dinosaurs. "Now that you're retired, you should come check out your old friends."

Sarah and Liam are the only ones who don't laugh.

> With liberty and justice for all:
> *with lips hurting / and just this / for all* — Michael Magee

The Twenty-First Century: Into the Second Decade

Irrelevant. All of it. The years I managed without a car. My efforts to use less gas. To cool the house by closing the blinds, to warm it by letting the sun stream in. To recycle as much as I could. And outraged. About having my irrelevance smeared across my skin the way the oil from the exploded rig in the Gulf of Mexico coated unnumbered pelicans, dolphins, tuna, shellfish, sea turtles. Plus beaches and tidal marshes and fishing boats and piers and the livelihoods of all the people who depended on fishing or tourism. What little oil they managed to burn off, the stuff that didn't pollute the Gulf and all its occupants, but instead turned into three times its weight in carbon dioxide, all by itself was the equivalent of adding half a million cars to the country's highways for a year. I might as well have been born a grain of sand for all the improvement my puny efforts had made in the world.

You have to understand I've spent a lifetime trying to be careful. I know how not to waste food, to make my own stocks, to repurpose leftovers. I grow my own herbs. I recycle plastics and glass and paper. I depend on the library for all but the most important books, the ones I need to have around me. I know how to buy clothes that last— sturdy classics that never look dated, at least not to me. How to save for retirement and invest in dividend stocks that grow over time. All irrelevant. Meaningless. Shown up for their paltry insignificance by a single massive instance of corporate carelessness. But no, that lets them off too easily. They couldn't care less, but careless doesn't begin to describe BP's behavior. How about care least? Or not a care in the world. Not a care for the world.

I couldn't stop wondering how many other irrelevant fools there were out there. "Maybe we need a Bureau of Foolish Statistics to keep track," I suggested to the poets.

"But who would want to use foolish statistics?"

"And how would we know in advance who or what would become foolish? Couldn't somebody foolishly track serious data by mistake?"

"Okay, you're not going to take me seriously. So what would Emily Dickinson do?"

Ardith brought the conversation back to poetry. "She'd write poems, of course. And she wouldn't worry about whether they were irrelevant. Or whether she was foolish."

We opened another bottle of wine and spent the rest of the evening revelling in the ways a line break can make a poem better, more allusive, less linear. In this case irrelevant would be your word—whether you were describing the conversation or the ageing participants doesn't really matter. Although why would you bother, come to think of it?

Nevertheless, after that evening I found myself compelled to work harder at what I secretly worried was the greatest irrelevance of all—struggling to write short poems about big questions. Our jokes about a Bureau of Foolish Statistics reminded me of my delight at seeing my poems between the covers of a book, and our talk about line breaks—or maybe it was the extra wine—inspired me to think I could put together a new book of poems. Poems as spare as Emily's, that's what I wanted to bring into the world—the hope of writing even one single line as charged with possibility as *My Life had stood — a Loaded Gun —* drew me back to my desk every morning.

I devoted two drawers to my poems—the larger one was for poems that I wasn't satisfied with, that still needed work, and the smaller for the ones that captured my foolish insistence that every word should carry as much weight as possible. Even if the rest of the country lived for an excess that they didn't even know was Whitmanian—a parataxis of things, things and more things, stretching to the horizon, or maybe to infinity. And page by page, month by month, the stack in both drawers grew. On mornings when my writing went badly, I would sort and resort the imperfect poems, and the worst ones descended into a folder that I opened only when I remembered a line that I might be able to steal for a better poem. But the best mornings happened when a poem came together in a way that qualified it for the small drawer.

Then, just as I was gaining poetic momentum, I found myself caught up—obsessed, to be honest—with the Occupy movement as it spread from Wall Street to Berkeley and Oakland and San Francisco.

"Finally," I said to Alex, "people are realizing that income inequality has gone way too far,"

"Do you really think that any of this will make a difference? As far as I can tell, they're planning to let the protesters blow off steam for a while, wait until the media get bored with it, and then they'll send in the police."

"But they seem so determined—and I love that they're trying to model a new approach to decision-making—that they give everybody a say. It all feels so hopeful."

"If you want my opinion, I think it's hopelessly idealistic—and that's what's going to kill them. There's no coherent agenda—they're getting attention because it's new and disruptive, but if you were in government, what would you offer them, even if you wanted to? They don't know what they want."

I didn't want to argue. Instead I decided I'd check it out for myself, see how I could help. Not in Berkeley, where the students already had rational demands and didn't need me to help them, but in Oakland, which felt closer to the seductive ideals that were on display on Wall Street.

I spent the morning making sandwiches, labeling them so that people would only take what they wanted—egg salad, ham and cheese, tuna salad—and packed them in an old picnic cooler, together with a stack of juice boxes. Apple juice. Orange juice.

The juice boxes were a mistake, I realized, as I trudged twelve long blocks from the car, lugging the cooler, first in one hand, then the other. In the end I just clutched it to my chest with both arms.

Another mistake was ignoring upper body exercise for too many years, I thought, determined to go deeper for the root cause of my fatigue. At last I arrived at the plaza, arms trembling. My body tried to compensate by panting, but then my lungs rebelled against the smell of garbage and smoke and sweat that hung in the air.

A huge crowd milled about. Men and women, mostly young, although not all. Black, white, Latino. Towards the center of the crowd people appeared upbeat and happy. Even the police who were farther away from me seemed more or less relaxed. But in the area where I had arrived there was an uneasy tension in the air. A dense line of well-armed cops, all male, arms folded across chests bulked out by their protective vests, looked exasperated beneath their riot-gear helmets. They eyed the protesters as if daring them to step out of line. Something had just happened, or was about to happen.

A hulking young man summarily grabbed the cooler from my arms, opened it, dumped everything on a table. Two sandwiches fell to the ground—he didn't bother to pick them up—probably didn't even notice. His eyes never moved far from the line of police. He shoved the cooler back into my arms. "See you tomorrow," he said. That was it. He turned to two other hulking males who needed his attention and said something to them that I couldn't hear. But I watched them brace their bodies, fold their own arms over their unprotected chests, and square off against the cops.

I guess I arrived at the wrong time. Definitely at the wrong place. Given the size of the crowd, my sandwiches and juice boxes, even though they were heavy enough to make my arms tremble, didn't matter. I knew my anticipation of a thank you was old-fashioned and bourgeois and probably even counter-revolutionary. So I took my empty cooler and retreated, leaving both the protesters and the impassive line of cops behind. Maybe I should have enlisted Ardith and the poets—we could have arrived as a group—we would have been braver together. How foolish to think that I would make a difference all on my own.

Anyhow, it was done. I suppose I could have pushed farther into the crowd, talked to someone with less pressing problems, shared my support for what they were doing. But I didn't. I knew I wouldn't come back again. I felt too small, too old, too useless. And too intimidated by the threat of violence. I plodded back to my car, lugging the still awkward weight of the cooler, fighting the temptation to put it down and disown it. You're almost there, I told myself. Just a half a block more.

That was when I saw the woman. Not a protester, just another of Oakland's homeless, with her long, messy hair and dirty clothes. She was leaning against a grey car, mine or the next one, I couldn't tell. Her skirt was pulled up to her belly, she had no underwear, her feet were braced on the curb. And she was peeing.

I screamed across the distance between us. "Stop that! Stop!"

"What's the matter with you, lady? Haven't you seen anybody piss before?" She laughed at me. She had a horrid mouth, mostly toothless.

I was closer now, and saw that her naked butt was up against the door of my car. I grabbed my keys from my pocket and turned on the car alarm, let it do the screaming for me. She finished peeing and dropped her skirt, turned her back and limped away from me without so much as a dirty look. Her backside had left a smear in the car's coating of dust and her pee was a disgusting puddle. I climbed into the car from the passenger side.

It wasn't until I was merging onto the freeway that I found the answer to her question. Not on a car door. Not in broad daylight. Not a woman on a car door in broad daylight. I discovered I was crying.

"The whole thing was so humiliating," I said to Ardith as we shared a pot of tea that afternoon. "From start to finish. I'm embarrassed to tell Alex about it. Even if he didn't say I told you so, which he wouldn't, I'm sure he'd be thinking it."

"Whatever will you do when he retires and you don't have a couple of hours to pull yourself back together before he gets home?"

"Stop doing stupid things would be a good start."

"It wasn't stupid. But maybe you're not cut out to be an activist? And maybe your timing was unfortunate?"

"The scariest thing was that horrible woman. It felt like she was a version of me from some awful parallel universe. As though my revulsion implicated me too."

"That's interesting. Do you want to expand on that?"

"You sound like a shrink. And no, I don't. But what the whole day made me think about was how we—the whole country—are turning into the polar opposite of what we were, or at least what we aspired to be. On a basic level that goes far beyond politics, it feels to me like where we used to be mostly xenophiles, celebrating the melting pot, however imperfectly—when we welcomed the other, when we cheered for the new and the different and the underdog, but now we're afraid of all that. I worry that we're turning into a nation of xenophobes—that the fear and hatred are winning. The cops today all looked like they hated the otherness that the protesters represented. And the protesters looked at the cops in the same way. Even us—you and me and Alex and the poets—we like to think of ourselves xenophiles, that we love diversity because it makes life more interesting, but if you scratch us—like that woman scratched me today—then our inner xenophobia rises to the surface and we can't do anything to control it. It was scary, Ardith. I don't want to be that person."

"You know, it could also just be bad luck. If you'd stayed with the crowd longer, or if you had parked the car a little farther away, none of this would have happened. And you wouldn't be in a state."

"So you're saying it's all my fault?"

"Of course. Who else's fault would it be?"

We must have already been on the verge of laughing when Alex walked in the door and thanked me for getting the car washed.

Because your main public face during those years was the occasional soft-focus headshot of a younger you in Cancer Foundation ads, I never found out what you thought of either the BP oil catastrophe or the Occupy movement. But the next year, when Hurricane Sandy slammed the entire East Coast in the days before the election, you reappeared, newly packaged for Sunday morning television as the expert on how the hurricane would affect Obama's re-election bid. In retrospect it's laughable, since your earlier Hurricane Katrina coverage would prove to be an exercise in racist myth-making, but at the time, at least in the eyes of the media, you were the obvious go-to expert. You knew about hurricanes and you knew about politics, so why not?

On television you looked older than those soft-focus photos, but not that much. Those beautiful scarves helped, as did the restyled blonde hair. And make-up, of course. You appeared to be ageing gracefully. I don't imagine anyone noticed your jowls—we didn't know to look for them. More importantly, you could still spin your ratings magic—you always knew how to combine a series of well-packaged anecdotes so that they led to important conclusions, and you did it within television's time constraints.

You never once, though, drew attention to the enormous differences between Katrina and Sandy. Neither the easy conclusion that with a better president in office and better preparation for the storm, far fewer people died—to say that would have been to admit that Obama was more competent, which wasn't why you were there—nor the tougher conclusion that lives were saved because, this time around, the victims weren't assumed to be the enemy. You didn't tell a single story about cowering on the floor in the dark.

In the end, both hurricanes caused billions and billions of dollars of damage. But Katrina was the big killer—of lives (ten times as many) and of jobs (a quarter of a million jobs disappeared permanently after Katrina; Hurricane Sandy only destroyed eleven thousand). I tried again to write a decent hurricane poem—I wanted it to be part of my *Bureau of Silly Statistics* poems—but once again I struggled and stumbled until in the end I accepted defeat and moved on.

The crux of my problem was how to capture the elegant, understated racism that provided oxygen for the violence. How to gain imaginative entry to the rooms where decisions about who to help and who to hinder were made. How to gain access to the minds that held the assumptions that led to those decisions, about who to denigrate and demonize and demoralize.

"Poetry's hard," I said to Ardith over yet another pot of tea. She filled both mugs, slowly, without a single drip, while her face revealed a struggle to find something helpful to say about my poem.

"Of course it is. If it were easy, everyone would be a poet."

"Life is hard, yet everybody does their best to live. So maybe everyone is a poet in their own way. Do you remember what Audre Lorde said—I'm not sure I've got it right, but something like 'for women poetry isn't a luxury, it's a vital necessity.'

"Well then, you're a woman, so isn't it time you worked harder at your poems? Since it's vital?"

"But I'm doing something wrong—the words arrive dead on the page, if they arrive at all. Missing in action describes it better." I crumpled up my poem and threw it towards the wastebasket.

Ardith looked guilty. "It wasn't that bad."

"It was exactly that bad."

Nevertheless, taking Audre Lord to heart, every morning I returned to my poems. And gradually they evolved into something close to a finished manuscript. Along the way I discarded the *Bureau of Silly Statistics* title and replaced it with *Just This*, which I borrowed from Michael Magee's riffs on the Pledge of Allegiance. Because, as I explained to Alex and Ardith, since we're apparently incapable of achieving justice, let alone justice for all, even after hundreds of years of lip service, at least we can still create a poem. Or own this present moment, however flawed we and it are.

We celebrated the finished manuscript with fresh crabs and champagne, and then I started sending it out to various publishers, each with a heartfelt cover letter that reminded me of Finn's applications to all those colleges back when he was looking for a place to teach.

Nevertheless, despite all my effort, despite all the support from Ardith and the poets and Alex, despite everything, the manuscript languished. In physical and electronic inboxes. Nothing happened. Other than a thin string of rejections when publishers took the trouble to respond at all. Thank you for your submission. Which is not a fit with our publishing program. But we wish you all the best. Sincerely.

Then, just a few days ago, I belatedly realized why my poems were being ignored. They were wrong, starting with my notion that writing a poem is an act of creativity, that a poem could be a force for good—that a poem could at least be a reminder that greed and fame and dominance are insufficient reasons to be alive. I was outdated. Out of tune with the times.

You probably haven't heard about Kenneth Goldsmith, the peacock of a white male poet who sent the poetry world into paroxysms last week, but it's a big deal among people concerned with poetry. Here's what happened. Goldsmith, as well-known for championing 'uncreativity' as for his flamboyant outfits and Walt Whitman beard, was invited to participate in an Ivy League symposium called Interrupt 3. On stage, he read a version of Michael Brown's autopsy report—Michael Brown, the unarmed black teenager killed by a cop last summer in Ferguson, Missouri. A killing that spawned riots and the Black Lives Matter movement. Goldsmith had edited the autopsy report because, as he said, "I always massage dry texts to transform them into literature, for that is what they are when I read them." Somehow that gave him the literary license to shift the following line to the end of his reading: *The remaining male genitalia system is unremarkable.* "To enhance the poetic effect," he explained.

The arrogance—on top of his tone-deaf appropriation and distortion of the underlying document—is breathtaking. Since it comes out of his mouth, therefore it is literature. QED. And he's been getting away with it for a long time—once he recorded every word he spoke for a week and turned it into a published book. (He didn't bother capturing the responses, which were the words of other people and thus not literature.)

His audacity got him invited to read at the Obama White House, where he turned a weather report into a poem by—you guessed it—having the words come out of his poetic mouth. It got him appointed the Museum of Modern Art's first poet laureate—all because he has defined uncreativity as the ultimate in creativity, because this is new and improved conceptual poetry, and because he is his own best salesman.

But let's go back to the symposium, which was rendered speechless by a half hour performance informed only by Goldsmith's presumption. Some of the unremarkable audience—only seventy-five people—must have remembered that today, in 2015, Black Lives Matter, because over the next few days the blogosphere and the Twitter-sphere erupted with condemnation and counter-condemnation, all of which, as far as I can tell, will only expand our white male poet's fame.

Goldsmith, with faux modesty, claimed, "I don't write anything new or original . . . . A child could do what I do, but wouldn't dare to for fear of being called stupid." With less modesty, he asserted that his autopsy performance was "powerful." What many people thought was that his performance had reduced poetry to a reality-television poetic lynching.

The lessons for poets who want to be published are clear. Uncreativity is the new creativity, especially if you call it conceptual. An outrageous, exploitative, so-called poem—plus a poet who indicts any reader who responds to it as moral human being—is what's needed to break through the general indifference of arts consumers. Being a peacock helps. And forget about bothering with a Black Studies course or two before committing an act of racially fraught uncreativity. It would only get in your way.

The lesson I took to heart was to stop trying to get published. A decision justified and verified by the arrival of another rejection of my manuscript on the same day. Or maybe the next day. Thanks but no thanks. We prefer uncreative conceptual nonsense. Sincerely.

I let my anger simmer offstage. I wasn't brave enough to tell anyone about any of it. Not Alex. Not Ardith, who remains blissfully unaware of the surging importance of uncreative poems. They would only try to jolly me out of my decision, try to prove me wrong. And definitely not Joy, who would ask me why I ever bothered with something with no payoff. But from here forward, my poems—the ones I can't help but write—are for me and the people I love. I'm sixty-seven years old, I have a gifted grandchild and a resilient herb garden, and I refuse to subject my poems to the world's rejection. Even though I know my refusal is pointless.

And then, with the kind of timing that could almost make me believe in divine intervention, the news of your public humiliation arrived in yesterday morning's *New York Times*. The story itself—alleged fraud—hints of corporate malfeasance—possibly involving cancer victims—questionable board appointments and potential kickbacks—plus the promise of more revelations to come—Cynthia, it's balm for my chicken soup soul. And best of all, there were those jowls, hanging from your face like Christmas ornaments and raising my spirits.

Of course I'd be the first to admit that arriving at sixty-seven without jowls doesn't rate as one of life's key accomplishments, but at least I did it without resorting to fraud. Just healthy living—fruit and vegetables and lots of fresh air and exercise—not a single facelift in my past. Which makes me wonder—why didn't you take those jowls of yours under the knife? Surely you have enough money for a facelift? Why not turn your face into a fraud too?

After all, if even poetry can succumb to the all-American appeal of transgression and violation in search of more attention, why in the world would you of all people stop at just make-up and hair color and beautiful scarves? Not to mention fraud—allegedly.

But I'm repeating myself—time to stop. This time around, the bard of baseball doesn't get the last word, because the former national pastime is also sinking into irrelevance. Instead, let's take this opportunity to celebrate a poet who is creative and insightful, who is black and beautiful, and whose genitalia, remarkable or unremarkable, belong to her and her alone, and not to any other poet.

You are a uselessness beyond my myopia — Harryette Mullen

FRIDAY, NEAR MIDNIGHT: New York City

It's very late and you still can't sleep, despite the second bourbon you allowed yourself, the drink you savored drop by drop, as if it were the last one before prison. You turn the light back on, see the tangled results of all your tossing and turning, and admit to yourself that sleep is impossible.

Instead, you once again worry about your pretend interview. It doesn't look any better, despite the remnants of bourbon in your system. If anything, it now looks worse, although that might be your mind playing games with that big X you drew through the money section. The upshot is that you no longer feel you can deliver those lines with the requisite authenticity. And as you know only too well, without one hundred percent sincerity, it will fail. Not a B, not even a mediocre C, but a big red F.

Your gut tightens as the anxiety rises. The word 'frantic' is thrown to the top of your mind by the churning surf in your stomach. It refuses to sink back to wherever it came from. You need to do something or it will only get worse. Should you call your lawyer? Not at this time of night. You don't qualify as an emergency. And even if you could reach him, he would only hang up as fast as possible.

A friend, then? After all, you know so many people, most of whom refer to themselves as your friends. And they're good for lots of things—peopling a party, donating to a charity, making introductions, schmoozing over lunch—but do you trust any of them to have your back? Your ex-husband, the man you never called Pink? Or Brown, if you still knew how to get in touch with him? No, and no. There's too much history there, in both cases, and besides, they haven't been in your life for a very long time. Old lovers are the wrong choice, the wrong place to look for help.

A woman, then. But not Barbara Jordan, who's dead and wouldn't like you anymore if she weren't. Not Barbara Walters, who's not dead but who's too old and besides which, she doesn't like you either. Former mentors probably belong in the same category as ex-lovers—not available, not reliable.

Childhood friends? Could one of us—possibly even me—be trusted to listen, to offer advice instead of judgment, to keep your secrets instead of broadcasting them into the gossip-sphere? Assuming you could remember our names and how to get in touch with us? No, we too are part of the detritus you've left behind without a pang of regret as you, with such perfect resolution, kept your eye on the future, on the main chance.

Xanax, you think. There must still be some in the bathroom. From the last time. You remember the blissful descent into calm. The possibility of a good night's sleep. It will probably still work.

> I pledge allegiance / to the flag
> *hype ledge a lesion / to deaf egg* — *Michael Magee*

FRIDAY, NEAR MIDNIGHT: Berkeley, California

"Look what I found—how in the world did Sarah manage to miss the best wine of the evening?" Alex is ecstatic, flourishing the bottle of Stag's Leap chardonnay that Joy and Liam had donated to the feast. "Forget about the dishes. They're mostly done anyhow, and I'll do the rest in the morning. Promise."

He pours the remainder of the wine into two glasses and we settle into the swivel chairs in the bay window. I feel more content than I have all day. "This is delicious, isn't it? Poor Sarah—although she definitely had enough without this."

"And she didn't need the best to get the effect she was after."

"Anyhow—lucky us." I look into the dark beyond the window and wonder whether this is the right time to tell Alex about my latest rejection.

Instead, I shift to Joy and Liam. "Do you think they're headed toward divorce?"

"Evidence?" Alex, as always, goes straight to the central question.

"The sniping tonight—it reminded me of Finn and me—they weren't listening to each other—they were just trying to score points."

"They've been doing that for a while. Although I think Liam more often backs off—more flight than fight, if you like."

"You're right—and that withdrawal too reminds me of me—what I did when I stopped caring about Finn and gave up on trying to make it work—long before I admitted to myself what I was doing."

"You know that there's nothing we can do?"

"That's what makes it so sad. I don't think Joy has any idea what's happening—she's still in the if-only-Liam-would-get-with-the-program phase, while Liam, I think, has moved to the why-do-I-bother-to-care phase. And neither one of them is wrong—but neither is right either."

"Is that a benefit of growing old? That we can see both sides?"

"If it is, it's a wasted benefit, don't you think? Because it doesn't come with any special powers to fix anything. It just reminds you of your own uselessness."

"But seeing both sides—that has to help your poetry, doesn't it?"

That's when I tell him about the rejection and about how I should have been writing uncreative poetry.

"I've finally figured it out," I tell him. "It's not poetry that matters, despite what Ardith and I have been saying all these years. It's fraud. It may be the only thing that matters right now. Most obviously when you get caught—front page headlines and Twitter and all the gossip. Like us taking Cynthia apart at dinner tonight. But I think fraud matters even more when powerful people get away with it and prosper. How they use greed as an accelerant and go on to bigger frauds. And that's why things keep getting worse."

Alex does his best to cheer me up. He even jokes about your upcoming indictment, about how that will be a blow for truth, justice, and the American way.

"No," I say. "Right now it feels like justice is as outdated as creativity. Joy was right—she'll somehow wriggle out of the whole mess and this will all be forgotten."

I drain the last drops of my wine, savoring the taste of not quite sweetness. I'm left with an empty glass and an unpublished manuscript. Oh Emily, I can't help thinking. You were so right. Keep your expectations low and keep your poems in a drawer.

And just this / for all — Michael Magee